ZANDER
&
ELLA

W. WINTERS &
AMELIA WILDE

WALL STREET JOURNAL & USA TODAY BESTSELLING AUTHORS

Playlist

Sweet but Psycho - Ava Max

Turn Down for What - DJ Snake and Lil Jon

River - Bishop Briggs

Unsteady - X Ambassadors

Overwhelmed - Royal & the Serpent

Are You with Me - nilu

Sit Still, Look Pretty - Daya

Scars To Your Beautiful - Alessia Cara

Issues - Julia Michaels

From USA Today best-selling authors W Winters and Amelia Wilde comes a sinful romance with a touch of dark and angst that will keep you gripping the edge of your seat ... and begging for more.

I should have known when I couldn't keep my eyes off her that this would be a mistake.

I was hired to protect her, this woman who's lost everything yet there's an obvious fire that blazes behind her beautiful gaze. She stares back, daring and tempting me. It calls to a side of me that's darker and longs to tame her.

We both have secrets, we both have a past we're not ready to face. More than that, we both want to get lost in each other, falling into a forbidden game of control and power. Of submission and dominance.

The moment she agrees to my terms, I know I've crossed a line. One of many rules I'm willing to break. No one can know, not a soul, but secrets in the life I lead never last for long.

KISS
ME

PROLOGUE

My mother used to say, "If you can't stop thinking about someone, it's because they can't stop thinking about you either." It bears noting, though, that my mother was a fucking lunatic. She stalked a man and killed his wife because she was in love with him. Having no idea, he married her and shortly she became pregnant with me. It wasn't until years later that he discovered the truth.

I was only seven years old when the trial was broadcast.

Cameras rolled and my sadness was caught on film. With interview after interview, journalists said the nation was entranced. As my fairy-tale life fell apart, what was left of me went viral. Every household knew my name, and the public begged for more. More of my twisted life; born into wealth and power, yet the daughter of a murderer. More of who I was.

My first kiss was photographed and the images sold to every major tabloid.

The first time I had sex, the world knew immediately after.

I talked about it with everyone.

I didn't know any better.

It's simply the way it was after my life imploded. I lived for sharing everything about my life with my followers, and they loved me for it.

I made my own happily ever after, and then it was ripped away.

In a single moment, my life changed forever.

I broke. There was nothing left after I'd loved and lost.

And then he came into my life in a way no one else ever had.

He was my protector, my therapy; he became my everything.

It's a dangerous situation for so many reasons.

I'm starting to believe the things my mother used to say … which scares me because I know I've already broken down and lost everything once.

But when he looks at me like that …

When he tells me it's going to be all right …

I believe the things my mother used to say. *If you can't stop thinking about someone, it's because they can't stop thinking about you either.*

Chapter 1

Zander

The Firm is an elite, full-service private security company for high-profile clients and those who require the utmost discretion. Please inquire directly for assistance with booking. All sensitive matters will be handled with complete confidentiality.

There are two things I can't stand for anyone to be when they enter a courtroom: late or rattled.

Being late never looks good, but people get lax about it. They tend to brush it off. What's a few minutes in the grand scheme of things? Could be nothing.

Could be everything.

Could be everything.

As for being rattled—there's no place for emotion in

a courtroom, not from my position. Calm, logical ... even ruthlessly cold is far preferred over rattled. Being focused is a personal rule of mine no matter what a judge says or what some lawyer pulls out of his back pocket. Not coincidentally, steady focus is also the number one rule in my profession. When we're with clients this directive is absolute.

I don't slip up when it comes to this charge. There are other areas of my life that require strict focus. The last time I slipped up, there were consequences.

I was late. I was rattled.

Today, hurrying up the wide stone steps at the county courthouse, I'm both late and rattled, which only serves to piss me off even more. The bitter autumn wind bites against the exposed skin on my neck as I grind my teeth and pull open the heavy floor-to-ceiling door after rushing up the marble stairs. I hustle as quickly as I can to make up for lost time, while still keeping my pace and gait professional.

The entire time I scold myself, adding anger on top of annoyance.

And it gets worse. The hearing today is an important one for The Firm. It's the most important hearing we've ever attended, according to my brother Cade.

I rush through the metal detector and snatch back my phone on the other side. The brightened screen's full of messages from my older brother. Cade owns the company; among other businesses, he created The Firm. He took on the responsibility of having the final say in which clients we take on, which is a hell of a lot harder than leaving it up to the group. He wants to know where the hell I am. With a steadying exhale I shake off everything from earlier this morning; namely, the hell of the phone call that lasted far too long. Rounding the corner and making my way to the elevator, I ignore the buzzing of my phone in my suit jacket pocket.

One last pause outside the courtroom doors to correct myself. I'm not taking the news from the phone call, and the memories that come with it, into work with me. I can't. That cursed entity needs to go back in the locked box where it lives most of the time. Calm focus. Eyes on the client. *Don't fuck it up.*

The door to the courtroom opens beneath my hand with a muffled squeak. Although adrenaline courses through my veins at knowing I'm surely disturbing the ongoing hearing, I keep my outward appearance unperturbed. It's one of the smaller courtrooms, which makes it even more obvious that I'm late. Nothing I can do about it now except stride in and take my place.

Damon's the only one to turn his head and watch me walk up the center aisle, even though the rest of the team's scattered along the last two benches too. Cade has a front-row seat to the proceedings. He's angled forward in his chair, breathing down the neck of the client's lawyer. Silas sits next to him, dark eyes trained on the judge, silent as usual. Dane's on his other side, with Damon behind him. Just as Damon and I make up a pair when it comes to relying on someone from the team, Silas and Dane have each other.

As silently as possible, I tuck in my tie and take the seat next to Damon, arguably my closest friend after the shit we've been through. He doesn't waste any time to lean over, pitching his voice low. "What did they say?"

My voice is deathly quiet when I respond, "I don't want to talk about it." My blood chills at the recollection and the back of my throat dries up. I don't want to think about a damn thing that involves that call. Sure as hell not right now.

Damon knew the call was this morning. I'll tell him the details later. For now, I need all my attention on the back-and-forth between the judge and the lawyer. This conversation is why we all need to be here. Our presence is proof we can handle this particular case and client. It's a deal that will set this company down a path my brother has been after for years.

I scan the judge's face. He's familiar and I know him by name. The wrinkles around Judge Martel's eyes and his thinning, combed-over white hair are proof of his experience on the bench. Ever self-possessed, with his lips pressed in a thin line, it's impossible to decipher which way he's leaning. My gaze quickly moves to the back of our lawyer's head, and then—

A pair of dark eyes.

Peeking at me from up front.

Instantly my body heats. The depths of their darkness stir something inside of me. The stunning stare is both intoxicating and pinning. As if I've been caught. But not by a predator, by prey.

It's only a moment that our eyes meet and lock, but something thumps through my chest like a heavy book falling to the floor. Then she faces the judge again.

The client. She's the client. Eleanor Bordeu. Born into wealth and a high-profile individual, but I hadn't even seen a photo of her. The simple white blouse that drapes along her curves is obviously expensive, yet it doesn't compare in the least to the woman who wears it. "Strikingly beautiful" would be putting it mildly. Her elegance is in the details; from the way she holds my gaze, to the manner in which she breaks it just as easily, squaring her shoulders to retake her place before I interrupted.

The moment is gone as quickly as it came and I surreptitiously clear my throat, adjusting in my seat.

Bringing me back to the present, Damon presses a thick folder into my hands. "Maybe you should read the file this time. The rest of the paperwork came in this morning."

I accept the folder but keep it closed and lay it on the bench beside me. "You know I'm not going to do that." I speak just above a murmur, as does he. Both of us are careful not to disrupt the hearing.

He noticeably shrugs. "I know. Cade wants you to have

it anyway."

My gaze instinctively moves back to the client and I rub a knuckle into my chest to try and dispel the lingering shock from … whatever the hell that was. A strange anomaly. Not something that ever happens with clients. Not something that ever will again. I drag my focus back to the hearing at hand.

"—client is only being held because of a temporary lapse of judgment. We believe this is an appropriate transition out of institutionalized care."

The judge turns over a sheet of paper, the mundane sound carrying through the quiet room. "There's mutual agreement between the parties, yes?"

"That's correct," answers the representative for the Rockford Center. His name is Aiden and from what our lawyer tells us, he's more than happy to comply. He stands a few inches shorter than the lawyer, his thick head of hair at odds with the crew cut the lawyer wears. I've met our lawyer a few times now. He's a good guy, which is rare to find in that profession; at least it seems to be that way since we've come to New York. We've been working with him on this transition for at least a year now. In our line of work, it's beneficial to have a lawyer on retainer. In our case, it's a whole team of hotshot lawyers, given the profile of the clients we take on. Cade is well versed in the law and has kept up with his license to practice, even though he graduated with his JD and passed the bar ages ago. Still, we rely on the best to represent us and

Cade is more than willing to admit the legal team we have is better at what we need than he'll ever be.

"The Rockford Center is prepared to relinquish custody to The Firm." My spine stiffens and I sit straighter as the judge scans us in turn.

I'm certain the judge is aware this is a first for us. The Firm started as a high-end protection service. Given the team's background and expertise, we've pivoted recently in our niche. It's not something I agreed with, and this situation ... this isn't what I signed up to do years ago. But here I am.

From my experience, some judges have piss-poor poker faces, but not this one. I can never tell what he's thinking. That uncertainty is only reinforced as Judge Martel scans the documents in front of him. "The Firm has representatives present, I see."

"We do, Your Honor," answers Cade as he half rises. His tone is professional but his deep baritone still gets the attention of the judge as if he's caught off guard. My brother, and boss, continues, "We are more than happy to answer any questions or address any concerns you may have in order to help make your decision."

"Mr. Thompson, the Rockford Center is prepared to relinquish custody. Have you been made aware of the requirements for this transition?"

"Yes, we have, Your Honor."

"Are you prepared to present your plan for the client's

home modifications?"

"Absolutely, Your Honor." Cade stands fully and passes a stapled stack of papers to our lawyer. He takes them up to the judge, but the client—Eleanor—doesn't move. She's so still, her chest barely rising and falling with each breath. I search for subtle movements in the curve of her neck, in her shoulders. Her hair is twisted into a prim bun at the nape of her neck. She appears quite polished, but also as if she's scared for any bit of her presentation to go astray. That's exactly what it is, a presentation. If I had to guess, she's been in this position before. Maybe not in front of a judge, but in some other way.

This is why I don't read client files before I meet them. What you see on paper doesn't tell you what they need. Half the time it clouds your assessment. The black letters on white paper don't do justice to the grays of morality. Every shade matters because they all come with a story. A reason. A thread that makes up the fabric of who they really are when no one else is looking.

I trace a path down the loose, white shirt she wears to her slim-fitting black dress pants. The shirt has a keyhole detail at the very top on the back of her blouse, a few inches below the dark twist of her hair.

Before I can stop myself, before I can swing my attention back to the judge where it belongs, I think of touching her there. My fingertips on soft skin. Would she shiver? Would she lean back into it?

As if she can hear my thoughts, she turns her head and her somber gaze meets mine.

Oh, shit.

I yank my eyes away from her. Back to the judge. Outwardly, I'm wearing a professionally neutral face. Inwardly, I feel the hum of an electric shock. That phone call shook me up more than I thought it did. It's not the client. Not Eleanor. My reaction has nothing to do with her.

The judge finishes reading Cade's plan, detailing what's already been done to accommodate the guidelines, and the mood in the room shifts. "Mr. Thompson, do you have adequate personnel to ensure two individuals are on hand around the clock?"

"We do, Your Honor."

"And you're equipped to provide appropriate security?"

"Yes, Your Honor."

"The Rockford Center has signed off on the proposed plan of care?" The judge's eyes flick to Aiden. The man's navy blue suit hangs well on him. With his slicked back hair, it's hard not to notice he took great effort in his appearance for today.

"We've met extensively on the proposal. The Rockford Center has full faith in The Firm to provide care."

The judge taps the papers with his knuckle. "I'd say we've moved beyond providing care and into full guardianship. I've never signed off on a transfer of custody this extensive.

Your company will not only be responsible for providing personal care. The level of mental health services needs to be comparable to, or exceed that of the Rockford Center."

"Your Honor, we are equipped to provide those services." Anyone else would think Cade was sticking to the rules of engagement—calm focus. But I'm his brother. I see the tension in the side of his jaw. He wants this to go well. We all do. And not just for the company.

I've made it a point not to know all the details of Eleanor's past. She deserves a clean slate with me, just like any other client. But the situation itself is different. The judge isn't exaggerating when he says he's never done this before. There's never been a custody transfer from the Rockford Center, or anywhere like it in the state, to a private company. Eleanor's case will be the first.

"If it's a matter of documentation, Your Honor—"

The judge waves Cade off. "This is a matter of character." He looks Cade in the eye. "You assume all of the responsibility for this patient's care. You also assume all of the risk. The state will intervene if there's cause to believe you're not meeting your obligations."

"Understood, Your Honor."

The judge shuffles his papers again; for once, the gentleman is showing his nerves. "Does the Rockford Center have any additional input?"

"Only that we've vetted the plans by The Firm and have

full confidence in Ms. Bordeu's care. The staff at the Rockford Center all agree that the institutional setting has served her to its natural endpoint. It's time for Ms. Bordeu to return to her home. Under appropriate supervision, of course, and getting all the care she needs."

With a simmering strain, the courtroom awaits the judge's verdict with bated breath. I hold mine, keeping with it the pent-up tension from the call this morning, the guilt I feel over being late, and my burning, driving curiosity about Eleanor Bordeu.

There's a small movement at the front of the room that grabs my attention.

Eleanor's eyes, flicking toward mine.

This is the third time she's looked at me. The third time those dark eyes have pinned mine. It's as if we've met before, but we haven't. I would remember a woman who looked at me the way this woman does now.

Only one other woman has looked at me that way.

The memory of her tiptoes across the back of my mind. She had blue eyes, not brown, but the curiosity was the same.

Eleanor drops her gaze to the floor, and I remember to breathe.

The judge considers each of us in turn. "What you've requested today is unusual. So unusual, in fact, that I've considered denying the request to change custody simply to avoid setting a dangerous precedent. But you've impressed me today, Mr. Thompson. You and your team." An exhale leaves me as he waves the papers in front of him, held in a loose fist. "I'll grant your request to transfer custody and care of Ms. Bordeu from the Rockford Center to The Firm, with the full understanding that a life is at stake. Perhaps many lives."

A shiver moves over my spine. Judge Martel referring to future cases with future patients makes me uneasy. If he opens the door to Eleanor's custody transfer, then it's open for more people after her. He and other judges will have to preside over cases like this one, but there will be precedent—us. I know that's what he's talking about. But the words "a life is at stake," combined with the phone call, feel like ice at the center of my gut.

The conversation continues but dims and seems to blur into nothing as I stare ahead absently. My attention is on my own pulse. Steadying myself and refusing to allow any unwanted emotion to surface. I can't meet the rest of this day with a knot in my stomach.

I can't meet the rest of this day with the delicate curve of Eleanor's neck on my mind. Or the way her sleeves flutter near her wrist in a simple, classic detail that makes me want to trace her bare skin there all the way around.

I can't, and I won't. I will not think of her that way. Not ever again. She is beautiful and tempting, but she is not mine to have.

With the pen held tightly in his hand, the judge signs a

paper in front of him and taps his gavel in a perfunctory way that seems anticlimactic for all the work we've put in. As soon as his decision is finalized, there's a flurry of motion. Aiden leaves his place at the front first. "Quick call," he says on his way past. "Then I'll be available." The lawyer nods, and with a thin smile his hand lands on our client's shoulder, gaining her attention. A heat rises up my chest, but it's quickly displaced. Cade leans over the partition to talk to the lawyer. Silas and Dane get to their feet next to him. Then Damon. I'm quick to follow, taking great care not to give much thought to how slowly the lawyer's hand drops back to his side.

Eleanor bends to lift her periwinkle wool coat from where it sat folded over her chair and pulls it on over slim shoulders. My palms ache in the strangest way. Like I should be helping her into that garment.

She doesn't look at me as she dutifully follows her lawyer out of the courtroom.

Damon's hand comes down on my shoulder, giving me a short squeeze. "You ready?"

CHAPTER 2

ELLA

The Firm will provide each client with twenty-four-hour care and security. All clients' needs will be identified and addressed by the partners directly.

There's an emptiness that's unsettling. I've stood in this exact spot more than a dozen times, taking in the sight of this home. One of several I've lived in over the years, and truthfully, it was once my preferred home although with everything that's happened, it was never an option for it to be more than a refuge.

I don't believe that places can be haunted. Haunted houses and such ... I've never given much credence to the notion. Do I believe in ghosts? I do ... ever since I was a little girl. That sense of wonder and shiver of fear never left me. I think we all do to some extent; it's simply a matter of what has happened to each of us that leads us to believe.

But I've never thought that ghosts can haunt a physical place. My aunt, who I haven't seen in nearly a decade now, once told me that spirits don't haunt locations; they haunt people. She told me there was no such thing as a haunted house.

She said lost spirits follow people who they miss, the ones they have unfinished business with, or a long-lost soul they wish would remember them. So I've never been scared of ghost stories. After all, my mother and father didn't want a damn thing to do with me when air still filled their lungs; surely they didn't give a shit about me once they were buried six feet under.

Never once have I felt the presence of any being ... But as I stand in the foyer, I can't help questioning my beliefs. Every corner of this house seems to hold a memory that's desperate to come back to life. Even with my eyes closed, the laughter from events long gone echoes in my mind as if it's all so close. As if I could reach out and my hand wouldn't meet cold air and proof this home has been vacant for nearly two years now. If only it was so easy.

No. My aunt wasn't right about spirits and ghosts.

There are no haunted houses; there are no ghosts at all. There are only haunted people.

"When was the last time you were here?" The deep

timbre brings me back to the present and the voices go silent. There's only a creak of the floor as my memories slip away back to the corners of my sorrowful mind. I wish they would stay. I wish I could go back to them more than anything.

With a shaky breath blown out from between my slightly parted lips, I bring my eyes up to a kind gaze, although behind it is intention.

"I'm sorry," I respond respectfully, taking in the fact that I am not at all alone, although it certainly felt like I was for a moment. For a very long moment, if I'm honest; too long of a moment. "What was that?"

The gentleman named Cade is the owner of a company my manager holds more confidence in than I do. I focus on his rather large hands as he forms a loose fist to clear his throat again. He's nervous and for the life of me, I can't understand why Kamden put his faith in him. Once he's done clearing his throat, he repeats his question. "When was the last time you were here?"

Letting out an exhale that's far from easy, but for his comfort, I allow it to be seemingly casual, I respond, "Over a year." He tucks in his tie, although his deep green eyes never leave mine. There's kindness there. He's professional but kind. I add, "Maybe two by now." My voice turns raspy at the last two words. I'm still recovering and I've barely spoken for the last few months as it is.

There's been no one to talk to. No one I've wanted to

hold a conversation with either. For a moment the memories of laughter and happier times threaten to come back and instead I hold the poor man hostage in a trivial conversation.

Gesturing to the nearly empty space, I tell him, "Last time I was here we furnished the foyer with the rug and bench, and I intended to finish the space ..." my voice trails off and I don't bother finishing. With my chest feeling hollow, I remind myself that I don't owe them anything. Not an explanation, not an answer.

"We can work on that, if you'd like," he offers and it takes me a moment too long to understand that he's referring to picking out furniture for this far too large house.

Nodding, I take a half step back, my cobalt wool coat providing the only warmth I feel as it's draped over both my arms that are crossed in front of me. "We could start by turning on the heat?" I joke, keeping my cadence as smooth as I can and my voice gentle, to make up for my tardiness in comprehension. As if on command, there's a click of the furnace that's undeniable, and rather unsettling.

The white macael porcelain flooring is elegant and fresh, but is at odds with the vintage, pale and distressed medallion rug I chose years ago. The entirety of this home consists of shades of creams and dark blues. Modern furniture with retro accents and polished copper details only add to the iciness of the mountain setting when we came here to ski for the winter. It's a careful mix of hard and soft, but I never realized until now just how cold it all is.

My initial instinct is to start fresh and redesign everything; I used to love doing that. Donating what's here and bringing in new pieces, playing with color and all things from the newest collections. My teeth bite down on the tip of my tongue at the thought. A moment flashes before my eyes as I stare at the thick rug, and I know then I'll never replace a thing that graces this home.

"Is there anything you'd like before we start?" he questions me. I have to lift my chin to look up at him. I'm rather tall, all legs so I've been told, but this man with his broad shoulders is even taller. He resembles the other man in the courtroom, the one whose dark gaze pinned me more than once. A chill runs down my spine at the thought, although the rest of me seems to heat with anxiousness.

"I think I'm fine for now," I offer with a tight smile I'm all too aware doesn't reach my eyes.

Silently, Cade nods.

One breath in, and he offers to take my coat for me. One breath out and he leaves my side. It feels like all the warmth in the room leaves with him although he's only a few short feet away.

The din of chatter drifts toward us and muddled within is the familiar, confident pitch of my manager. Giving orders as he always does.

"Shall we?" Cade asks and again, I question everyone's

decision. His. Kam's. Even the judge.

I'm not certain he knows what he's getting into, especially after the court hearing. I don't know what he knows about me or what research he's done. I imagine all he's been presented with is the file Kam gave the Rockford Center. Which is as barren as this empty foyer.

Lord knows there's plenty on the internet for him to find, but none of it is what truly matters.

My heels click as he leads me through my own home to the sitting room across from the open kitchen. I wonder if he judges me as I judge him. I wonder what he thinks, the wheels turning as he interacts with me. Am I what he expected? I used to be able to tell from the first time I met someone what they knew about me. The men were the easiest.

A smirk was almost a given if he'd happened to stumble upon some of my younger days online. The corners of my lips lift slightly at the knowledge.

I know there are still a few … risqué videos … still lingering on the web. It's possible he's watched those, but if he has, he doesn't let on. Perhaps, though, what's happened most recently far outweighs the past.

I have to consciously stop my racing thoughts before the spiral begins and it's then that I notice how the chatter has stopped.

"Ella." Kam's voice is the first I hear as I take in the group of men. He's already taken off his suit jacket. It's hanging over the back of a mahogany stool with navy blue tufted upholstery at the kitchen island. The kitchen is a stark white with the same porcelain tiles as the foyer to my right, but the dark navy of the stools is echoed to the left, covering the walls including the wainscoting and coffered ceiling.

"Finally." He announces the word with his hands up, arms outstretched. His charming smile greets me just before he embraces me. Kamden's never been a large man and he's always had a smaller frame, but like me, it appears he's lost weight. His jawline shows it the most.

I vaguely wonder how else he's been affected. I know his boyfriend left him when I was first committed. He wasn't well then either, but in the months I've been away, I haven't heard from him apart from his plans to get me home.

In my heels, I'm eye level with him.

"Finally," I repeat, echoing his upbeat and relieved tone. It does wonders for my mood. To see him, to hold his hands and know I'm safe. To feel truly protected. This man would move mountains for me. He has before.

"How are you feeling?" Before I can answer, he lifts a brow and comments as he moves to the sitting room with me trailing behind him, "It was fucking freezing when I first got here. How the hell do we turn this fireplace on?" If his tone is anything to go by, today is any other day and the last year didn't happen.

Oh, how I wish. All the wishes don't add up to anything I

can hold on to, though.

The silence is uncomfortable as all the men in the room watch me, all six of them, and the only thing that can be heard are my heels muted by the rug as I slip across the room to flick the switch to the gas fireplace. It ticks steadily until it lights, and then blue flames rage from the crystals.

"Ah," Kam says, then claps and makes his way to stand beside me. "What would I do without you?"

His calming and comforting voice only eases the brokenness slightly. His genuine smile produces fine lines around his eyes that I never noticed before.

"It's been a cold year," I tell him and my throat turns tight.

"It'll warm up soon, babe," he replies and quickly turns, no doubt in an attempt to hide any true emotion that brought the glossiness to his gaze. If he thinks I didn't see it, he's mistaken.

One breath in, one breath out.

"I'm sorry it took this long." His apology grabs my attention and I catch his gaze skipping from my collarbone back up to meet mine when he asks, "Have you eaten?"

Self-consciously, I reach up to pull the blouse back in place.

Cade cuts in before I can answer that I don't think I've eaten since this morning. "Should we discuss the menu that was suggested—"

"Absolutely not, she can have whatever it is that she wants to eat. There's no reason that she can't," Kam cuts him off, responding with a strictness that he's always had. Ever since I was a teenager, when my dad died and Kam took me in to keep me from going to the state, I've never wanted for anything a second longer than it took for me to tell Kamden what it was I'd set my sights on.

Whether it be food, drugs ... a man. He's the brother of my long-time friend Trish, although I haven't seen her in forever. He's a good friend, a father figure in some ways, but in all things, my rock. If I'm honest, I felt most comfortable with him more than anyone else simply knowing his preference for men. I could tell him anything, show him anything, and he would never use me as other men had tried. Hiring him as my manager was unquestionably the easiest decision I've ever made with my estate. Recently, he's also become my conservator.

"Everything was a misunderstanding and that place did more harm than good," Kam says, meeting my eyes rather than Cade's or the other men in the room I've yet to be introduced to.

A misunderstanding. The very word steals my breath.

"What'll it be?" Kam asks, ready to take any order I give him and, in my periphery, Cade watches the two of us. I don't miss the skepticism. Kam's gotten me out of trouble for years. Never anything like this, though.

"I think I'd like to go over the necessities and meet these ... gentlemen first?" I state, turning slightly so I'm facing the room. With the fire blazing just beside me, my back is to the corner. As the sun sets beyond the paned windows, the fire casts a shadow along the man standing the closest to me at the end of the long white couch.

The roaring flames seem to dance a little hotter as I take him in. His white collared shirt is tight over his broad shoulders. I'm not certain if it's the lighting or something else that makes him appear even more intimidating in my home than he did in the courtroom. There's a tension that crackles, an undeniable feeling that's nearly suffocating as I force myself to meet his stare and not to back down. His eyes are gorgeous, a concoction of shades of emerald and ambers, his jaw chiseled as he remains where he is across from me.

After a moment he nods, acknowledging me for the first time.

I dare to speak, barely breathing. Interrupting whatever is brewing between Kam and Mr. Thompson, I comment, "Let's get on with it," and with that I break this man's gaze to turn to the room again. "Shall we?"

CHAPTER 3

ZANDER

All partners of The Firm have extensive backgrounds in high-profile security and personal client care. We are equipped to respond swiftly and appropriately to any need or crisis.

Ms. Bordeu stands through Cade's introductions the way she stood through the hearing—still. Her delicate hands folded in front of her. Next to the fireplace in the sitting room where we've gathered, with her manager, Kamden Richards, close by her side.

Maybe I imagine that she glances at me a moment longer than the others.

Maybe I don't.

Unlike in the courtroom, it's my job to watch her now. I'm required to do it. Required to observe her reaction to everything. So why does it feel so damn forbidden?

There's a tension I can't shake, no matter how much I ignore it and focus on Cade. The gentle ticking of the clock seemingly intensifies as every second passes, as does the need to loosen my tie. Clasping my hands together, I ignore the heat that threatens to suffocate me.

I can't ignore her, though. Every small sway of her body, every nod at Kam's interruptions, every time her eyes glance down and then land back on me. Holding me there, daring to look away. I'm never the first to break our shared gaze. She's always the one who closes her eyes and, once they're open, directs them on someone or something else.

It doesn't feel like a job right now. It feels like a peep show. As if studying her face for every tiny reaction is something forbidden and off-limits, not the thing I'm being paid to do as part of The Firm.

Cade doesn't allow silence after the introductions are made, and summarizing the mundane details from the hearing goes on too long. "Now we'll need to go over protocol, Ms. Bordeu. Would you like to take a seat?"

It's a smooth transition, meant to put everyone at ease and direct the client's attention. But when Eleanor's eyes slide to mine, ease is the last thing I feel. Calm focus has gone to hell and brought the heat back with it. Tension tugs at the air between us. It's written in the set of her slightly parted, pouty lips. My thoughts tussle with lewd desires that shouldn't be anywhere on my mind. This situation is never a comfortable one, the introduction of a client and reviewing their specific needs from us. It makes sense that she's uncomfortable. Especially given her mental health, which is why we've been called in. It's not protection from a stalker or a former coworker or lover ... It's protection from herself, from what I can gather.

It makes sense that she may feel on edge. Skeptical, perhaps. Saddened or embarrassed by the entire ordeal given the excuse her manager continues to state: just a misunderstanding.

But ... that is not at all what I gather from her reticence.

It's my eyes she looks into, far too often, with wariness a dull flare. It makes my palms itch to touch her. To comfort her in a way no professional should ever do. Once again our gaze is broken, but this time it's due to my brother walking the length of the room as he closes the folder of paperwork, satisfied there were no issues with the general outline of our arrangement.

This woman is in our care as she resides in her private domicile. We will see to it that she receives the same level of care as she was before, including twenty-four-hour surveillance. The evaluation of her treatment will occur at regular monthly intervals by Mr. Aiden Miller the representative of the Rockford Center, along with an approved concierge doctor. Which means we will be here with her for a month, at minimum.

Cade claims a seat by the fireplace and gestures for Eleanor to take the one across from him, then Dane and Silas sink into two free chairs. Damon positions himself behind Cade's chair, leaning against the wall by the fireplace. Kamden hovers in the open archway between the sitting room and great room, positioning himself to observe although I have no doubts that he'll be the one speaking on her behalf. He's already taken that initiative.

Across from all of them, and farthest away from our client, I lean against the wide, black windowsill. This way, I see her in profile. This way, I'm not staring into her eyes.

Professionalism is required and I am a damn professional.

Eleanor lowers herself into her seat and I twist the top off my water bottle. My mouth has gone bone dry, heat prickling at the back of my neck. This woman, in this room—it does something to me.

In this light, I see more of her, more details she's hidden. Her haunted eyes and too-slim wrists are on display. In the first moment, as everyone gets comfortable, she reaches for her throat, only to brush her fingertips over it and then put her hand back in her lap.

It's as if she's out of place in her own home. A home that reeks of luxury and wealth. Old money she was obviously born into.

Her gaze flicks to various places in the room, no doubt noting the changes we've made. Even though the room is clearly kept spare and clean, there are pieces missing. Items we took out. No bottles of alcohol wait in the gleaming bar stand in the corner. The picture frames have had the glass removed, which was one of the many recommendations we received from the center.

As I lean back, feeling the cold windowpane against my back and grateful for the chill, I remember how opposed to this I was. I fought Cade and questioned his decision. There wasn't a single desire in me to babysit an affluent woman who didn't want to receive her care in a private institution.

The Firm has a background in law and psychiatry, but we're known for our military experience. We're more than just professional bodyguards, although that's what I'd prefer we stick to. Cade's vision for transitioning this company isn't why I signed up to be on his team. I wanted an adrenaline rush and as little interaction with the clients as possible. He wants to move into a more high-end, private and potentially gray market.

There wasn't a dollar amount that made me lean in favor of his decision.

Now that we're here, I understand the intrigue and the desire for a more complicated situation.

Cade lays the folder in his lap and shakes out his arms.

"If you don't mind, I'd like to roll up my sleeves and get comfortable with the particulars," my brother says, directing his statement toward Eleanor. She merely gives him a thin smile and nod in return.

"We should be through this quickly, starting with the schedule." He launches into the shift rotations and designated meeting times, followed by how any items coming or going, including any shopping, will be handled.

That, and more, until Eleanor interrupts him. Her soft voice cuts right into an explanation of the around-the-clock care services we'll be providing.

"I'm expected to talk to you?"

"To talk to us?" Tilting my head slightly, I wait to hear Eleanor's response to my brother.

Her hand goes to her throat as if she needs the physical support to get the words out. My eyes narrow as she swallows thickly. It hurts her to speak. I'm sure of it. That knowledge makes the hairs on the back of my neck stand up. "You want to conduct therapy sessions in addition to the mandated monthly sessions from the center?"

"That's correct," Cade answers. With his hands folded, he leans forward and looks her in the eye. That's my brother. He doesn't flinch, doesn't shy away from other people's discomfort. "It's essential that we're involved in your care. We cannot help you or protect you if we aren't included in each aspect that's questionable when it comes to your safety."

"I think you'll be rather disappointed." Eleanor's voice is low and strained, like it's been brushed with steel wool. "I haven't much to say." There's a note of melancholy that's tangled in her nearly dismissive response.

"As part of our agreement, we need to offer on-demand access to emotional support."

Eleanor's manager, Kamden, pipes up from the archway, his tone hopeful. "Therapists will be coming and going. You'll meet with them as well."

She glances incredulously toward him, the corners of her mouth tugging down. But then her dark eyes come back to Cade, back to his attention. Eleanor nods without speaking, seemingly accepting the terms against her will. More questions are asked, this time from Cade. Her responses are short. Occasionally she follows the lead of her manager, searching him out before answering.

It's like she's conserving her words. What makes her choose one moment over another to use them? I give the manager a once-over as Cade moves through his agenda. I don't know what to think of him. He prefers to go by Kam, and that's the sum total of facts I have on hand. Obviously, he makes his money off Eleanor. I have questions. Like what happened to her that she ended up like this—withdrawn and wary and broken—and he appears to be just fine and speaking for her more than she speaks for herself.

The fourth time Eleanor's fingertips grace the dip of

her throat, Kam interrupts to offer her tea. She nods and I anticipate that being the only response, but she adds "please," just above a murmur.

Their relationship is ... unique. Something about him doesn't sit right with me. I file my skepticism away for later.

Damon takes a half step forward from where he stands to the left of the fireplace as Kam turns on his heel to head to the kitchen, and my brother's focus follows him. Leaning forward, he meets Eleanor's eye level. She observes him with both curiosity and hesitation.

He softens his expression to question, "Everything all right so far?"

Her nod of acknowledgment comes with the faint sounds of Kam's efforts to make the tea just behind us in the kitchen. "Damon, right?"

He mimics her response with a nod in affirmation, offering her an asymmetric smile as well. "That would be me." Damon's dark skin is complemented by his cobalt blue suit that nearly matches the walls, and his smile is as white as the shirt he wears under the slim-cut jacket.

Giving him a simper she relaxes slightly, although there's still the tension that would be expected given the situation.

"I want to put your mind at ease," Damon continues. "Each of us has received training in emotional support, and I am a board-certified physician." A psychiatrist, to be exact.

Her smile wanes and the light in her eyes dims. For a

moment, I think she's not going to respond, but then she explains, "What if I don't want to talk at all?"

Again, a nervous prick travels down my spine as Damon jokes with her that he's comfortable in silence. It puts her at ease at least. That or the tea Kam offers her.

"Are we good to continue?" Cade asks just as Kamden gives Eleanor's shoulder a light squeeze and returns to his position.

Taking a brief swig from my water bottle, I get the attention of Dane and Silas who have yet to speak, but luckily it doesn't distract anyone else.

"I think it might be helpful for you to record your thoughts to share with the therapists at the Rockford Center. Either by writing them down or recording yourself. That way, you could maintain a connection with them, even if it's through videos."

Eleanor's shake of her head is firm, although her eyes are luminous with anguish. "I don't want to talk to a lens." Every word out of her mouth feels carefully weighed. As if she's balanced them all against the pain it'll cause her to use her voice. "I've done that enough."

"Ella," Kam's tone is pleading. He takes three long strides into the room at the same time that I speak.

"I like to talk." I ignore the burning look I'm aware Cade is giving me. "I've got stories to share if you want to listen. Maybe share some with me?" There's a note in my offer I wish wasn't there. A smoothness in my tone, casual and inviting, that I don't use with clients. One I hope the rest of the men don't pick up on.

Clearing my throat and standing up straighter, I cover my tracks, motioning toward Damon as I add, "It can be easier to share in group settings."

They all stare, even Eleanor. I'm aware of every inch of my body. Of my too-casual lean against the windowsill. Of the water bottle that's seconds away from being crushed in my hands. I loosen my grip on it and meet her eyes. A semblance of a smile lifts the corners of her mouth. My lungs feel tight from holding my breath. I don't let it out. Don't even move. If she smiles right now, if that hint becomes something real, it'll be an accomplishment.

Eleanor's lips part, her brow arching as she eyes me, and—

"This will all be recorded?" Kam's voice takes the weak start to an inquisitive smile off her face and draws her eyes back to him. He's taken a step into the room to hover over her.

His comment is a rock through glass. Eleanor holds my gaze for another beat, and then it's back on my brother. Cade nods at Kam but then quickly returns his attention to Eleanor. "Of course. You don't have to stare into a lens. Cameras are already placed in each room."

The details continue without me as if I hadn't spoken at all, which is best. It takes great effort to ignore Damon's stare that burns into the side of my face.

It doesn't take much for her to agree. It's a battle she seems not to want to fight.

He carries on with the daily schedule, the rest of us shifting in our spots, listening along with Eleanor. My heart beats too fast for what this is. A status meeting, essentially. A way to get the lay of the land. Time set aside for all of us to be in the same room before we're on rotating shifts, in and out of the house, devoted to her care.

By the time Cade gets to the end of his list, shadows have fallen over Eleanor's face. The sunset is on its last gasp. It'll be pitch black soon. I peel myself away from the windowsill and reach for a lamp in the corner. With a gentle click, it bathes the room in a warm glow. Eleanor tips her face toward it like it's the sun and all I can see are the dark circles under her eyes. *What is it that keeps her awake at night?* At first glance, she was striking, although slender. Too slender. After spending the last two hours watching her, it's more than obvious she's not well. Kamden Richards is full of shit. It's not a misunderstanding.

"With that settled," Cade announces, "I believe that's the end of my agenda. That's all the information we have to give you right now. Was there anything you wanted to discuss before we call it a night?"

Eleanor shakes her head. There's plenty I want to discuss and unravel. Too much. I'm too curious, and I know it.

She's already standing when Cade offers to show her upstairs. She clears her throat with a hint of amusement. "I think I can find the way."

Cade gets to his feet, the rest of us hanging back although we're all standing now. I don't know what this woman's been through, but I'm certain she has no idea what to expect from us. Even after hours of going over details.

"This arrangement included minor changes to each room I'd like to go over with you." His tone is gentle, but not patronizing. Eleanor hasn't been through the whole house yet. She should be aware of the cameras and intercoms.

She seems to hear Cade's words a few seconds late. I see the moment they land. Her eyebrows go up, eyes widening, and her shoulders tense. If I hadn't been staring at her all this time, I might not have caught it. She begins to lift her hand but catches herself. "Not the west hall, though?"

Kam speaks up, his tone calm, "Everything in the west hall is untouched. Every room up there is just how you left it, Eleanor." Although his outward appearance is at ease, his grip tightens on the back of the stool. So tight, I can see the whitening of his knuckles from here. Kam's glance flickers to Cade when he adds, "I gave explicit instructions."

Heat trickles down my shoulders. Cade confirms nothing has been touched in that wing. We don't have access to it and neither will Eleanor.

Relief is exhaled along with her response. "Good." She mouths the word more than she says it. Eleanor crosses both arms loosely over her belly. She's still not comfortable—who would be?—but the fearful shine that flashed in her eyes is gone. Easing the tension out of my shoulders, I note that I'm left with more questions than anything after this meeting. So many that I consider reading the file. The idea lingers in the back of my mind.

"Let me walk with you upstairs?" Damon offers with an easy smile. He's muscular, as we all are, and the kind of guy you want to have in an emergency. I would know. He's helped me before.

Eleanor doesn't quite smile back, but she looks like she might simply to be polite. When Damon steps to her side she moves along with him, the two of them striding past her manager, who trails a few steps behind. He'll take her through the great room and into the foyer, and then they'll climb the herringbone steps.

Besides my brother, I'm closest to Damon. He's the one friend I could count on without fail in the last four years. Damon's a good conversationalist but given her sore throat, he's also comfortable with silence. There won't be a second of awkwardness between them.

Friendship doesn't do a damn thing to ease the possessive knot that coils my muscles as I watch him lead her away. Gritting my teeth, I force myself to look anywhere else.

This isn't like me. I'm not jealous, and I never have been. Let alone the unethical thoughts that have run rampant since I first laid eyes on her. Excuses come to mind and pile up, the most obvious being the call I took first thing this morning and how much that fucked me up.

Dane and Silas call me over to where they're standing, more than likely discussing the schedule and their thoughts of our new client. Holding up a finger and then the empty water bottle, I silently motion to the kitchen as if I need to throw away the trash before talking to them.

In the bright light of the kitchen, I steady my thoughts and my breathing.

It must be because Eleanor is not well. It makes her seem delicate. In need of protection.

Or in need of someone to take control.

All damned good explanations for why I feel like sprinting up the stairs after them, and for the same reasons I stay where I am, my mind shuddering away from the possibility.

I shake it off and come back to the task at hand. Cade has joined the other two men in front of the fireplace. I don't think any of them have noticed how scattered my thoughts have been. Or how the majority have been focused on Eleanor in a way they shouldn't. They'll notice if I keep this up, which I don't intend to do.

"Have you had a chance to read through the file?" Cade asks me as I join their circle.

"No. I'll get to it."

Cade doesn't push me on the lie. It wouldn't matter if he did. I want to hear her side of things. I want her to tell me what the hell happened to her.

CHAPTER 4

ELLA

*The Firm will provide for all necessary modifications
pertaining to the security and comfort of each client. These
may include, but are not limited to, home renovations
and the installation of complete monitoring systems.
Modifications are subject to change as the service progresses.*

My eyes burn as if I didn't sleep at all. Which doesn't make much sense given that last night I slept the most I have in months. It was off and on and took hours before sleep came for me, but still. I slept. A dreamless sleep, thankfully.

I'm busy rubbing my eyes when I hear heavy footsteps walk into the kitchen. I'm grateful my back is to whomever it is so they don't see the exasperation in my expression.

I'm grateful to be out of the center, grateful for my own bed and an ounce more privacy, but I'd like a moment from under the shadow of these strangers.

Gripping the cardboard box, I tilt it and the clink of cereal hitting the bowl is all that can be heard. The second the box is placed on the counter, whoever has joined me pulls out a stool from the island, the legs dragging on the porcelain floor.

If I didn't feel as exhausted as I do, if I wasn't grateful to be out of there and safe in a familiar place, I'd have contempt for all of them. Them telling me what to do, making changes to my home without my consent ... it's never sat well with me for a man to take control of my life. Other than one man.

"Morning." A deep baritone interrupts my thoughts, soothing them and giving me a much-wanted distraction.

Taking my time, I peer over my shoulder, ignoring the warmth the sight gives me. His broad shoulders pull the collared shirt tight as he leans down to reposition the stool once again and then takes his seat. He opted for a burgundy shirt and black jeans today. The dark tones bring out the flecks of gold in his hazel eyes.

Zander is a handsome man in a traditional sense. Although he's clean-shaven today, I most certainly prefer the stubble he came with yesterday. His hair is short on the sides, but there's plenty to grip on top. His tanned skin is a stark contrast to how pale I've become. I'd guess from his appearance he worked a blue-collar job, not this.

His last name is the same as Cade's—Thompson—and I wonder if he's related and that's the only reason he's here.

"Good morning," I offer him and ignore the raw pain at the back of my throat. The doctor said I needed to practice speaking again to lessen the vocal strain. After the surgery, I could barely speak for weeks. But then again, I could barely do anything for weeks.

"I didn't expect you to be up this early," Zander tells me. His name and his promise to tell me his stories kept me company as I lay in bed last night. I believe I remember each of the men's names, but Zander's is by far the easiest.

"I never met a Zander before," I comment rather than offer up my dry humor with the accusation of how he could possibly know what to expect from me. After all, I haven't known him for twenty-four hours yet; I probably shouldn't risk offending him.

"Well, I'm glad to be your first." The corners of my lips tilt up at his drollness. Perhaps he would have liked my joke after all. He adds quickly, as if second-guessing his choice of words, "How are you this morning?"

"My throat hurts," I whisper but it goes unheard as I pour the milk into the cereal.

"I'm sorry, I didn't hear you," he says.

After putting the milk back in the fridge, I move the ceramic bowl to the island across from him and answer politely, "I'm all right." I mean to ask him how he's doing too, but my throat burns; the cold milk is too tempting not to drink some of it first.

In my silence, Zander says, "I'll try not to be obvious."

"Hmm?"

"I'll give you space while I'm here."

"Oh," I say and the word falls flat from my lips. Loneliness creeps between us.

"Unless you'd like the company," he offers. It's kind of him, and obvious that he only offered because of my despondency.

"I thought you had stories," I murmur, peeking up at him from beneath my lashes. There's a quick spark, one that frightens some side of me I'm not yet ready to confront. It's too early for such things.

A tall disposable coffee cup hits the counter and I stare at it, rather than the prying gaze that fuels the heat rising into my cheeks.

"We could share stories," he states lowly. A prick travels along my skin as the tips of my fingers numb. The sugary puffs that float in the bowl come with memories. They dare me to tell Zander why, for two years, I made sure this cereal was always stocked.

At that recollection, I push the bowl away from me. The porcelain protests as it drags against the stone.

"Do you want something else to eat?" I meet his gaze as he adds, "I'm no chef, but—"

"No," I say and then clear my throat, hating that the

simple act makes it hurt that much more. "I'm fine." What a lie that is. A lie I'm sure this man can read as easily as the written words on the back of the cereal box. I debate pulling the bowl back and eventually give in, my hunger winning out. It's the smallest things that bring me to the edge. Something as simple as a brand of cereal.

"You all right, Eleanor?"

"Call me Ella ... please."

"Ella," he echoes, seemingly testing out my name, his deep voice caressing each syllable. It stirs something inside of me, something that buries my previous thoughts, making me grateful for him repeating my name.

There's a quiet moment before he picks up the conversation again.

"What kind of music do you like?"

With a smirk I think the topic is one step above asking my opinion of the weather. Although given how kind he is, and how pleasant he is simply to look at, I'd talk about whatever he'd like.

"All kinds," I tell him and finding my own answer lacking, I elaborate before he can respond. "I have two favorites I used to listen to: "Heart Attack" by Demi Lovato and "Sit Still, Look Pretty" by ... I forget who sings it."

I peek over the counter at where he's seated to find an amused expression.

"Daya, I think."

I soothe each of the burning words with a spoonful of milk. My gaze drops to the streaks of gray that marble the pristine counter rather than holding his any longer. I haven't the energy to keep up with the pretense of yesterday. Regardless of my pride, he's practically my prison warden.

"You know them?"

"Not a clue," he answers and a bubble of laughter warms my chest.

He starts to say something, getting my attention but waves it off. "What?" I push him but he taps the empty coffee cup on the counter instead of answering.

"I have a coffee maker," I say, picking up the spoon and point with it, "if you'd like to make a cup."

"I'm fine with this. Thank you, though."

"You're a coffee drinker then?" I ask him. Yet another topic that's one step above the weather. Just doing my part in this ice breaking, I suppose.

"I am."

"Let me guess how you drink it." He grins slowly, taken aback by my tone. Even I'm surprised by the eagerness in my voice.

"Black with sugar. No milk?"

"Why do you think no milk?" he questions, not telling me if I'm right or wrong.

I shrug and he shakes his head. "Milk, no sugar."

"Oh," I say with mock dismay, "so close." I can't hide the

semblance of a smile.

"Let me guess how you drink yours?" he asks and I nod, biting down slightly on my lower lip. "Lots of sugar and no milk."

"You just took my guess," I say accusingly.

"You didn't say 'lots.'"

"Well, you're wrong anyway," I say between more spoonfuls of milk.

"So how do you like it?" he asks and my body reacts to his words as if the way he posed the query wasn't innocent. As if he was asking how I like something else entirely.

A mundane conversation with this man feels just as dangerous as playing with fire. Whispering, and not feeling any pain at all, I confess, "I don't drink coffee. I drink tea."

His eyes spark and it's in tune with a thump in my chest. Then I'm met with a rough huff of humor. "I knew that," he comments.

Even with the quietness surrounding us, I simmer. There's something about him that pulls me in, but there's also something that warns me to stay the hell away from him.

I've never been good at obeying warnings, though.

"Did you already eat?" I dare ask, interrupting the quiet moment.

"We bring our own food."

"That doesn't answer my question."

He gives me an asymmetric grin as my spoon clinks

against the bowl and I finish the last of my breakfast.

"Not yet. I'm waiting on Damon, you met him yesterday." When I nod he continues, "Once he's in, I'll be on my way."

There's no explanation for the reason I suddenly feel loss. I ask, "So you stayed last night?" and he nods. "What did you even do? Watch me sleep?"

The sexy smirk he gives me is utterly sinful. It's wrong that it sparks what it does inside of me. He nods and attempts a swig from his coffee cup but finds it empty.

I have to bite my tongue to keep from telling him that's what he gets. It's in this moment that I'm acutely aware of the attraction between us and how very wrong it feels. It's in the way he looks at me. How his stare seems to sink through me, anchoring me to him and holding me steady. He doesn't flinch, he doesn't hesitate, and there's a knowing challenge in his gaze. One that feels familiar although the man himself is very much a stranger who has piqued my curiosity.

My dry humor slips out in a deadpan mutter. "That's not creepy at all." I anticipate him laughing but he doesn't. I wish he would, I want to know what it sounds like from his lips.

I change the subject as quickly as I can, gesturing to his empty cup. "You sure you don't want to make another cup?"

Peering down at the nondescript cardboard cup, he hesitates.

"I don't mind giving to the needy."

He questions with humor, "Now I'm charity?"

I give in to the small laughter that comes with it and shrug. "Your words, not mine."

Instead of answering, he asks, "Cade said last night that you do charity work?"

The mention of Cade and the fact they were talking about me last night makes my throat go dry.

Nodding, I answer, "Kam says it's good for my image and I love it, so ..." With a familiar hollow sensation filling my chest, I take the bowl to the sink and pretend I'm all right. It's back to real life and no longer getting lost in the handsome stranger seated so close I can inhale his masculine scent. It's something woodsy yet fresh. Like a forest that rises above the coldest depths of the ocean.

The thoughts leave me without conscious consent as I say, "It's incredible the things people do. All they ask for is a platform, a chance. I'm grateful I can give them that."

"So you do charity? That's your ... thing?" I don't miss how his gaze sweeps over the expansive kitchen and past that to the sitting room.

"I don't make money from it, if that's what you're thinking." My brow knits and I question, "You haven't read the file."

"You know what's in there?"

I answer without hesitation, "Of course I do. Kam makes sure I approve it all."

Shock lights his hazel eyes, brightening them but he doesn't say a word.

Curiosity eats away at me until I ask him, "What do you know about me?" The suspense heats every inch of my body as I wait for an answer.

"Only what I've seen in the courtroom and at the briefing yesterday," he admits.

"And what Cade told you last night," I point out. I don't know why I feel so at ease knowing he doesn't know. I shouldn't feel relief, but I do.

"Yes, and that."

Something compels me to tease him as I make my way to the hot water spout, in desperate need of morning tea. "So you don't read the file and instead flirt with me in my kitchen in the early hours before anyone else is awake ... None of this sounds like conflict of interest at all to me."

The very moment I begin to second-guess myself, I feel his dominating presence behind me and when I turn to face him, I'm disappointed he wasn't there caging me in. Instead he stands two feet too far from me, tossing away his trash. A sharp tension snaps between us as the implications of what I've said hit me. The front door creaks open, alerting us to someone else's presence and Zander ends the conversation succinctly by saying, "So many interests. So many conflicts."

CHAPTER 5

ZANDER

Twenty-four-hour care is the standard for each client contracted with The Firm. A partner will be on the premises at all times, with additional detail on standby within a thirty-minute radius of the property. If at any time more security is required, it will be addressed immediately and without hesitation.

The door of the rented room sticks on my way in. Its resistance in the new autumn sunlight, slanting down the motel wall, echoes what I felt leaving Ella's house twenty minutes ago. There's a magnetic pull to her I can't fathom. She's a beautiful distraction who's mesmerized me. I could've listened to her talk all day, or even longer, about virtually nothing. It was as if a door had cracked open, letting in a little light. Her eyes hadn't seemed so haunted. Guarded, yes. Cautious—especially when Cade was mentioned.

This may be a different kind of case, but her reaction isn't unlike other clients. My reaction, though ... is certainly unusual. It's typical for our clients to react that way—relaxing a bit, once the initial awkwardness dissipates. Although I hardly interact with the clients. That's Cade's job. It's rare that I'm required to be social, and more than likely for the best. I'm a bodyguard, plain and simple. What makes our company, and our talents above the competition, is the attention to detail. The monitoring, the research. Knowing who the threat is and more importantly why. What motivated the need to call us. Emotions don't factor into it nearly as much as simply knowing people.

When it comes to Ella, though ... The first day has certainly been different from all the others.

My gaze drops as I toss the keys down on the barren dresser that doubles as a TV stand. It must've been a bit of a relief, sleeping in her own house with us to watch out for her.

I wouldn't know much about that. I've been alone for a long time now.

Inside the room, I close the door and lock the dead bolt. Cade secured a row of rooms in a mom-and-pop motel on the edge of the city. It's cheap but homey. Well cared for. You can tell the owners take pride in the place. My room has a queen-size bed with stark white, fresh bedding. A table and two chairs sit by the front window, the table decorated with a few stems of some pink flower in a vase. Fresh flowers, not fake. It's a nice touch, but the feminine flair is lost on me. They've repainted recently, because the new paint smell still lingers. I fall into one of those chairs and kick my shoes off, one at a time.

Alone.

Part of me relaxes at knowing there's nobody watching me. All night at Ella's, I felt eyes on my back. Maybe I was anticipating the moment she'd come down the stairs and say my name into all that quiet.

Maybe I was hoping she would do just that.

But Ella slept all night, and then this morning she lifted that spoon to her lips like it wasn't the most delicate, graceful thing I'd ever seen and told me about those songs she liked. I've already got them downloaded on my phone. They're already taking up space there, waiting for me.

Old guilt crashes in at the thought.

I let it hit. The waves bring exhaustion with it.

I can keep it shut out for the most part. I've had two years to learn to live with it. And I do live with it. There's no other choice. I'm alive, and I live with this hole, a wound, where someone else used to be. It feels like a deep gouge, but I know better. I've been to doctors about physical pain.

This is something else. Something I'll have for always.

Even the psychiatrist said so. Two little blue pills may help me sleep, but when I'm awake and conscious, that pain will never leave.

It's the pain of hesitation. Of the loss of strict focus. Once upon a time, I fucked up. I wasn't honest about what I wanted because I was afraid of the outcome.

Now, even thinking about exposing that truth—to anyone—feels like acid in open wounds.

Those wounds are best kept hidden. Tucked away like the words inside a closed book. Though I don't know how long that will work, either. Cade's been making noises for six months about how much time I spend on my own. I keep telling him that's how I like it. No demands on my free time, except for when I spend the weekend with Damon. We'll grab a beer every now and again. We'll work on some project or another. Go to the shooting range or gym to have company. He knows loss as well as I do.

Even Damon's made a few comments. I don't know what they want from me. I work for The Firm as much as I can, and in my downtime, I try not to think about the shit that almost destroyed me.

It might still destroy me. The heat kicks on as I unzip my duffle bag. Two suits are already hung in the three-foot-wide closet. I go through the motions of this part of the job without much mental effort, just as I have for the past few years. The job keeps me moving. The requirements are all-consuming. So I take them all. Falling into place and performing as needed. This one, though ...

It's more complicated, what with the news I got about the trial.

Stripping off my shirt, I drop to the floor and do a set of twenty push-ups. Then another. Followed by four-count breaths. Twenty more push-ups and the burn seeps into my muscles, stiffening my shoulders. I hold the position and do twenty more, faster, letting the heat break along my skin. Holding the upright position and then I break in another four. After eight sets the crush of guilt around my lungs eases up, and I head into the tiny bathroom for a shower. My chest rises and falls deeper, needing to steady, but my mind still races.

Turning the metal knob, the squeak of the old piping is followed by a spray of ice-cold water. By the time I've stripped down, steam has started pouring into the stall.

This, at least, is standard for missions. An affordable motel. A series of night shifts. I'm used to places like these, and schedules like these. I know how my brother prefers to put money into family businesses, local places that are less well traveled. I also know that he prefers contracts with clear end dates.

We don't have one this time. That's yet another difference with this mission. We're here as long as she needs me.

Needs us.

I work shampoo through my hair and try to ignore a

tension in my back. *You're in the wrong place*, it says as I stare blankly at bland white tile and let the hot spray batter against my chest. The fuck is wrong with me? My eyes close and I do what I can to shake the thoughts of her away. She doesn't fucking need me. She's only a distraction, although ... It seems as if she may need a distraction as well. Someone to listen to. Someone to talk to. Someone to tell her it's all right to feel whatever it is she's feeling. That thought is what breaks the dam. I can't stop picturing her sitting at the island in her kitchen, her bedhead swept back from her face and her eyes looking more alive for the first time, with a spark of mischief and the dare on her lips that there's no conflict of interest.

Tilting my face, I let the water splash there, condemning the disgraceful images that flick through my mind. I could so very easily get her to talk. One night with her and she would spill whatever it is that I wanted to know.

I can't stop picturing how she looked when she slept, one hand tucked under the pillow, her expression open and dreamy. I can't stop remembering the silence of her house. The expansive, open-concept space. All the room we'd have away from the outside world to—

To do nothing. We are not going to do anything. She's my client, and I am in charge of her care. I won't cross those lines with her.

But damn it, I want to.

I lean my head against the wall of the shower and sit with

this urge the way I sit with my guilt. I feel it. I feel all of it. My palms burn from not touching her. My arms ache from not folding her into them. Glancing down at my cock, I let out a huff of incredulity.

This situation is unbelievably fucked up.

Forbidden.

The kind of shit that could tank a career like mine.

Lathering soap across my body, the scent fills the room and I breathe it in, ignoring the baser instincts. I can handle this case and this woman, *Ella*. That's the only option, handle it like I've been trained. I ignore the ache below my waist, turn off the shower, and towel off. Washing the two pills down with water, I prepare to pass the fuck out and fall into a much-needed deep sleep.

Back in the small bedroom my phone stares at me from its spot on the table. What I need to do, more than anything, is sleep. I have to be fresh for the night shift. No dozing off when this case is still developing and all her secrets are still there, ripe for the picking. No slipping up because my mind is clouded with equal parts of emotion and want.

I snap the curtains shut over the windows and take my phone off the table. I'm not going to avoid the damn thing just because Ella's songs are on it. Other than a thin sunbeam slipping through the curtains, the screen is the only light in the room.

Stretching out on the bed brings a moment of relief. I

sink into the mattress and let my head fall back. Scrolling through the phone, I can't help that it feels loaded.

I know that downloading a couple of songs doesn't erase the past. It doesn't mean I owe less. It doesn't mean I'm moving on and betraying anyone's memory.

It doesn't.

And neither does the attraction I feel for Ella. Because I am attracted to her. Damn it, I am. I take in a long breath and blow it out to the ceiling. Unread emails stare at me from the small screen. Maybe I'm attracted to her because I'm looking for an escape now that the date for the hearing has been set.

The hearing has hauled the weight of the past two years right up to the present and parked it on my chest. This could be my mind's way of finding a way out from under it. Or at least a way to hold some of it up so I don't suffocate.

I shove the phone under my pillow, where I can't see it. It's dangerous to be having these thoughts. Dangerous to be having any kind of feelings for Ella. The whole damn thing feels risky in a way it didn't before I stepped inside that courtroom and those eyes met mine.

A harsh exhale brings me back to reality. She's nothing but a fantasy. Running my hand down my face, I remind myself that it's merely a lust-filled diversion and I imagine whatever pull she felt to me is the same.

Even entertaining the idea of more than a quick fuck with a woman makes my chest ache with that same scarred-over guilt. I hesitated before. Pushed back on the idea, and there were consequences to that hesitation. There are always consequences. It's twice as true now. If I can't get rid of these feelings for Ella, it won't just affect me. It'll affect the entire team, and especially Cade, who's trusting all of us with this.

I sling an arm over my eyes and swallow those feelings down. Wrestle them into something I can carry. Through sheer force of will I make the intensity fade, at least for a moment. At least for now. If it comes back …

I tried. And I'll keep trying, because this can't happen with Ella. It simply can't. I'm not going to put us in that position. Me. Ella. The Firm. I won't do it.

"The first days with a client can be like this," I say out loud, to no one but myself. I justify these thoughts, and why they won't turn into anything more than a delusion. There's an adjustment period. We're in that adjustment period, and it's more intense than usual because we've never taken on this kind of job before. We've never had a client with these needs.

I feel foolish, attempting to convince myself, but it's better than allowing this to get any further. Taking my phone back out, I stare at the two new songs, but scroll past them, deciding on a familiar melody.

I don't know what the hell I was thinking. Today was a mistake. That's exactly what Eleanor Bordeu is. A mistake.

CHAPTER 6

ELLA

Partners of The Firm will document client interactions and provide status updates to their team members at each shift change. Client records will be maintained by each partner and supervised by Cade Thompson, owner.

I haven't spoken a single word all day today. My throat hurts, but that's not why I've been silent and avoiding the other men from The Firm. Not overtly avoiding them.

I'm not trying to make it obvious, or draw attention to my mood.

It's because I want to save my voice for him. On the days my throat hurts, I save my voice for what matters most. And what matters most right now is talking to Zander. It's not something I can explain. It feels dangerous to talk to him. So risky that I know I shouldn't be doing it. And yet the sound of him—just the pure sound of his voice, the rumble of it over my skin—it made me crave more.

I've been craving him all day.

No, not him. Just talking to him. Just his presence. I don't crave Zander the man. That's not why he's here. He and the rest of the men from The Firm are here to protect me. To ... care for me.

I'm certain that's why I feel this need. He's obligated to care for me and he reminds me so much of the life I had before.

It scares the hell out of me, honestly. It's good to be home but it's terrifying in these ways I didn't expect. When I was at the Rockford Center, I knew things were bad. How could I not know? You don't go to a place like that unless the situation is dire. The rules there tell you exactly how bad things have gotten. Exactly how far you've fallen. People who are still holding it together don't need escorts to the bathroom or constant monitoring to make sure you're still breathing every night.

I woke last night, twice, when they came in to check on me. The creak of the door ripped my eyes wide open and just as I have for months, I woke with my heart racing. Thankfully, I don't remember what I dreamed, but I can imagine what it was. It doesn't take a shrink to point out the obvious.

They're still checking, the guys from The Firm. I know

they are. But there are no harsh lights, and no nurses shaking me awake in the morning, and it's my house. Which means I have something to lose. A height to fall from. I don't want to go back. I can't. All I can do in that place is remember. The white walls are painted with memories. The empty chairs are filled with ghostly visitors.

I won't go back. I'll be good. I'll listen. So long as they're here, I promise to behave.

Zander feels like a risk because he is. The warmth that moves through me when he looks at me, when he talks to me—it's dangerous with what it could do to me. He makes me forget it all. It occurred to me last night that it's because he doesn't know. I don't want him to know. If I'm only given the chance for a single line to speak today, it'll be a plea for him not to read the file. For him to keep looking at me as if he doesn't know I'm so unwell and damaged.

That's what my breath is saved for. It's why I'm still awake, fighting the pull of the medication I was given at dinner. It didn't go unnoticed that my pills are different here. Kamden told me what was changed, but I don't remember. Either way, I'm so damn tired. Too restless. And wanting.

I'm not sure what my emotions are capable of. That's why I was in the Rockford Center in the first place. I used to wonder what was so wrong with being emotional ... now I know.

The sun sinks below the horizon early, an autumn fireburst in the trees outside my windows. Dying light paints the blue sky gold and I drift between the windows, watching. The old restlessness from the Rockford Center creeps through my veins. It used to happen every night there. The sky would get darker, and my heart would beat faster, as if the night were something to be afraid of. I don't know why that happened. There were always lights on in that place.

Maybe I knew it was because that marked the point when I couldn't resist sleep for much longer. My worst fear was dreaming, remembering, and waking up screaming.

But this ... this is different.

My quickening heartbeat is the same. The urge to walk around, to pace, is the same. Only it's not anxiousness I feel.

It's anticipation.

For Zander to get here. I want him to arrive, to start his shift. I want to sense the danger in the air. I want to put myself near the risk of him. It's safe, although it seems the antithesis. I know it is. Maybe that's why I feel so brave, and so reckless. He has to protect me. He's obligated to.

With the warmth of the ceramic mug pressed against my palm, my gaze shifts from the handmade lantern seated near the covered porch to the stone driveaway. My heart races, although I don't show it. Damon's eyes are still on me, so I merely sip the tea and return to the blank notebook in my lap. Blank with the exception of the sketch of the lantern. It was a gift from my girlfriend, Kelly, on her last trip to Alaska—she thought it would suit my home perfectly, and she was right.

The light is brilliant at night, peeking through the varying sized holes of the glazed pottery. It creates a constellation against the dark wood roof. It's one of the things I dream of that doesn't bring the past to haunt me. Staring at the stars, imagining the northern lights I still have yet to see.

His car trundles down the street in front of my house at five minutes to nine. I take the interruption of the quiet night as my cue to stand, gathering my teacup to take to the kitchen. I allow myself a single glance before opening the large glass porch door. I can't see him, except for the outline of his shadow and his hands on the wheel, but every inch of my body tightens. Air flowing through my house caresses every inch of exposed skin. There's not much, what with my cashmere burgundy sweater and leggings. Headlights illuminate glimpses of the picket fence and the planters outside as he makes his way to the back of the house.

Where am I supposed to be?

My room? The sitting room? He'll come through the kitchen, through the door in the back entrance, and I have the urge to present him with a pretty picture. A relaxed woman, waiting on him. Exactly how he'd like me to be. The heat of my skin only adds to the untamed gallops in my chest.

But I'm not that woman. This is not a normal evening, and Zander's not coming home to me. He's coming to do his job.

I want him to do that job. Call me a sinner, or whatever name suits me best; I can't help what I want.

Striding through to the kitchen, I offer Damon a tight smile when he peeks up at me, checking as he's done all day. When I flip on the recessed lights over the stove, I'm certain Zander will know I'm in here, and I wait in front of it. The tap to the heated water begs me to fill my cup and I do, then add in a fresh sachet. Inhaling the comforting aromas of peppermint and chamomile, I do what I can to calm myself.

My heart pounds with the silence of the day and with Damon's prying eyes.

Damon steps into the kitchen as Zander's headlights cut off. "Is there anything I can help you with?" he asks softly. He's almost casual about it, the way he might be if he were a guest in my house and not one of my bodyguards. *Or prison wardens*, as my internal voice sarcastically jokes.

I swallow hard and summon up a sentence for him. Better to get warmed up now, before Zander comes in. "It's just a cup of tea, so I can manage, thank you." It didn't hurt much at all. If I keep my voice low, the vibrations limited, I find it doesn't pain me like it used to.

"You were fairly quiet today. I hope you know you can come to me whenever you want to talk."

"I do. Thank you."

"And the notebook? Is there anything you'd like to share?" he questions and my smile is genuine in response.

"I've done a poor drawing I wouldn't want to bother you with." My shoulders relax and with the rough laughter from the man across from me, I smile into the cup of tea. A cup that needs to sit longer so the tea can steep.

Damon's got an easy smile. He's not like Zander. Zander has a seriousness that follows him like a thundercloud. Like a dark suit, though he doesn't wear one when he's here. He wore a suit for court, but that's not what he wears on the night shifts. Dark jeans, and a long-sleeved shirt. Clothes he can be comfortable in. It was my request. I remember staring Cade straight in the eye when I told him I didn't want to be outdressed and they were putting too much pressure on me. It was a joke, but the poor man took it seriously until I apologized for my dry humor. I'm grateful he allowed the change in dress code. They still read as professionals, and it does put me at ease, a little more than before.

Cade is the most serious and the least inviting; luckily, he's also rarely with me. Damon's casual outfit of a plum button-down shirt and jeans puts me at ease. As does his warmth. He's kind, although I'm more than certain he's capable of brutality. They all are. Yet another reason for them to wear anything but the harsh professionalism of suits.

The comfortable silence is broken with the click of the back door opening.

Zander greets us on a breeze that carries the scent of night air and crisp leaves. The amber in his hazel eyes flares low in the dim light from above the stove, deep like whiskey in a glass, and those eyes burn into mine for a beat too long.

"Evening, Ella."

"Hi, Zander."

Damon crosses the kitchen to meet him, and the two men confer for a moment in low voices while I busy myself pretending to stir something nonexistent in my tea. I'm used to this. When they change shifts, they update each other on how the hours have gone. I imagine it's a boring conversation. Three days of this have passed and the most I've done is slept long hours, sketched in a notebook and stared at the sky from the lounge chair in the back.

Even through their lowered voices, I catch glimpses of their conversation. I'm welcome to add my own notes, but I haven't yet. My pulse races through the short update. I read in the sitting room, and I spent time in various areas of the house. Thinking and waiting. Waiting and thinking. Passing the long day. I know I'm supposed to begin therapy sessions with Damon. Or else the professionals will be called in, which I'd rather didn't happen.

But I *want* to talk to Zander. I'm curious what it would be like to hear his secrets. I'll show him mine, if he'll show me his. The wicked thought curls up my lips and my moment of perversion is cut short by the farewells between the men.

Zander reaches out and claps Damon on the shoulder, a warm, familiar gesture, and then Damon leaves with a wave directed at me. The way he glances between the two of us when Zander isn't looking is knowing, and it pricks my nerves. Not so much, though, as it does when Zander's gaze reaches me.

The door closes behind him and I breathe in a new magnetism. With that boundary between Zander and me and the outside world, it feels like anything could happen. Electricity runs rampant in my veins but I don't react to it, except to say what I've been waiting to tell him since I woke up this morning. "I'd like a session."

He blinks before narrowing his gaze, hazel eyes deepening in the shadows near the door. An almost imperceptible tightening around his mouth tells me he's surprised, but otherwise he doesn't let on. Zander stands straight and tall in his hard body, his hands at his pockets, his posture alert but not rigid. "Where would you like to talk?"

"The sitting room."

It's nearly a dance. That's what it feels like to me. A give and a take. Each judging the other with every small step. Maybe I give myself too much credit, maybe I'm carried away by it all, but it gives me a reason to want, and I'm unwilling to give that up.

Zander gestures for me to lead the way, then falls into step next to me. My heart climbs up into my throat inch by inch until it flutters there like a trapped bird. He's the one to enter the sitting room first, flipping the switch to turn on the fireplace and then moving to a lamp in the corner. It's not very bright. The perfect complement to the fire burning brightly in its grate. He sits in a chair facing away from it and gestures to the one across from him.

I take it.

This—this is uncomfortable. The moment I'm sitting I don't know what to do with myself, or with my hands, but old habits kick in and I fold them neatly in my lap. Zander takes this in. His hazel eyes see everything.

"Kamden says this should be filmed," I say, though we've been over this. We've all been over this. "This will be recorded, right?"

"Everything is being recorded." He nods and adds, "Always."

His confirmation sets something off in me. Something deep, and old. A desire I thought was long gone. A very specific desire, tied to a very specific memory. A warm bar. Fingertips on my jaw, on my throat, on the neckline of my dress. Heat glides up the back of my neck and wraps around to meet the warmth in my cheeks. "Not for the professionals." I offer a huff of a laugh. "Just if I want it."

Zander cocks his head to the side. "For you?"

"To share with people." I already feel exposed to him. I already feel like I'm telling him deep secrets, and I'm just saying what I want into the space between us. "I haven't seen them in a long time."

"I'm not sure exactly what—"

Zander's calm, even tone is interrupted by the sound of the kitchen door banging open. Kam moves through the house with heavy footfalls. He knows I'm still awake. We were texting not too long ago. But I don't understand why he's here. I didn't ask for help.

He makes it to the archway of the sitting room before Zander holds up a hand. "We've just begun a session." I don't miss how his grip tightens on the edge of the chair.

Kamden's blue eyes dart between the two of us and I don't miss how his left brow rises slightly. The man knows me well. Gently he asks, completely ignoring Zander, "Do you have a moment for me, Ella?"

He crosses the room and crouches down in front of me. "You sounded off. In your texts."

"I'm fine." It hurts to say things in irritation, so I try to pull it back, but it's right there. I can feel it. Waiting to spill out. "You could have texted if you were concerned."

"Or checked in with The Firm," Zander comments and it takes great effort to keep my smirk hidden.

"I wanted to check on you ... myself."

A tingle travels up the back of my neck. It's from a combination of guilt and unease. Kamden doesn't trust me. Not only that, but I'm certain the memories that haunt me have taken over a piece of him as well.

"I'm all right."

"You're sure?" he presses and the frustration is too great to keep my voice anything but tight.

"I have people here all the time." Like the man sitting

behind him, waiting to have a session with me. "If something were really wrong, they would know about it."

Still Kamden stays where he is, between the two of us, unmoving and not believing me.

"I promise—" I run frustrated hands over my hair. "I'm trying to do what I'm supposed to do, Kam, can you please leave?"

Kam's jaw sets. "I won't leave. You don't seem well right now, and I'm not going to walk away until I'm sure you're all right."

Anger fuels an uncomfortable heat that forces my body to move. Not only that, but pain. Am I to be punished and not trusted forever now? He didn't come to see me nearly as much as I would have liked at the center, and now he comes unbidden?

This is so ridiculous. So over the top. I get up out of my chair so fast that Kam has to scramble for balance. "Then I'll be going to bed. We'll talk another night, Zander."

I push past where Kam stands still with disbelief. All day. I've waited all damn day for this, and Kam has to rush in like he knows everything. He doesn't know everything. None of them do. Kam might know the most, but that doesn't make this okay.

"Ella," Kam pleads with me in a tone that brings about a renewed sense of guilt.

I don't stop. "Wait. Ella." I don't turn around, even

though it's Zander's voice behind me and not Kam's.

I get one foot on the bottom step and turn my head back to look at him. "Don't follow me," I snap, not realizing how close Zander is to me. So close my breath is stolen.

Zander's a foot away, maybe two. About to catch up with me. At my words his whole face changes into a commanding countenance. A hard one. A no-bullshit, no-nonsense expression that shakes me to the core. "Don't say that to me," he orders. "Ever."

Dominating. That's what he is.

And I like it. I like this about him. I crave that power radiating from him. It's as much need as it is desire.

I'm only vaguely aware that Kamden isn't in sight.

"Fine," I answer back. "Please, I want to be alone," I add and then turn on my heel and rush upstairs.

CHAPTER 7

ZANDER

As part of its protective detail, partners with The Firm may conduct research on clients using record requests or background checks with or without their consent so long as information is attained in good faith and kept strictly confidential.

The large house is quiet except for the wind battering the sitting room windows. That, and my thundering pulse.

I listen for her. Of course I do. I strain to hear soft footsteps on the stairs or even the creak of the floor above me, but there's nothing. I check the security cameras from my phone. No sign of movement, either in the house or outside. Silent and still. If only my heart would settle.

Not much chance of that.

The only cameras to watch are focused on her sleeping form. Even with the darkness, her luscious curves tempt me.

My exhale is uneasy as I lean forward, my gaze moving from the laptop to my phone. I occupy one of the modern white chairs in the room, while my phone sits on the one beside me. Those two fucking songs burn holes in it. As if they'll whisper more of Ella's secrets.

Snatching it off the chair, I put in a pair of headphones, and lean back in the chair. The laptop sits on the small coffee table surrounded by the four chairs. The screen is still very much lit and the cameras prove to show nothing of use. I blame boredom most of all.

So—the songs. I hit play on the first one.

It nearly blows out my eardrums. Cursing under my breath, I stab at the volume buttons on my phone until it's less skull shattering. I'm grateful at least there wasn't a soul present to witness that stunt. Readjusting in my seat, I take a gulp of water, wishing it were whiskey, and set back to listen to the first of the two titles Ella said were her favorites.

My brow lifts as the first one plays.

The song turns out to be ... cute. Even if it is about a love so strong it causes a heart attack. I prefer alternative to pop, but I can't say that I'm not surprised. It's the kind of song I wouldn't mind hearing on the radio, but not one I would turn to myself. Same with the second one.

Cute. They're cute, and maybe they used to reflect on her. Maybe these songs are an echo of the woman Ella used to be before the Rockford Center, and before we came on the scene. Before her "misunderstanding."

My eyelids get heavy with the beat. Not a usual response to pop music, I guess, but it's been a long night. My gaze finds Ella's sleeping form again. The prim and proper presentation she first put on are at odds with this melody.

She's not the kind of woman who listens to music like that anymore. Whatever happened to her has weighed her down. So much, in fact, that I can't imagine her dancing to this music. I can't imagine her with an infectious, broad smile on her face and a lightness to her step.

I could, though …

My eyes widen as the thought strikes me. The information on Ella is out there, as evidenced by plenty of social media posts. Maybe even videos on YouTube or in the depths of Google. If I wanted to spend five minutes searching for it or reading her file, I'm sure I could find plenty of information regarding Ella's former life.

At this point, I'd have to go with a broad internet search. I lean toward that over the paperwork Cade gave me. If the file has been heavily curated by her manager, which Ella hinted at before, then they'll have left out any unsavory matters. Let alone instances in which "Heart Attack" and "Sit Still, Look Pretty" would rear their jubilant heads. It won't be the whole story. Nothing will be the whole story—not without Ella telling parts of it. But I could get hints. Glimpses of what she was like before.

It would mean going against my own personal code for clients. It would mean crossing another line, even if Ella never knows. A hundred justifications fill my mind, but the one that shouts the loudest is the one that's desperate to know a side of her that may be lost forever.

Tossing my phone down, I bring the laptop back in front of me and my thumb taps softly on the space bar. I don't dare press it. I don't do anything but flick through the cameras once again. Hating that there's nothing to watch but her. A woman who already occupies too much of my mind.

I take my time with a few more checks to confirm that everything is under control—and that Ella isn't coming back down—and I finally settle on scratching that itch and sating my curiosity, opening up a tab to search her name. There's relative privacy in here to conduct my "research."

It's not unusual to investigate the pasts of our clients when necessary. Most notably if their story doesn't add up. It used to amaze me how many lies we'd be told that only added to the threat. As if they'd rather die in a lie than live in the truth. This, though … this type of search is unwarranted. My entire body knows this search is different, from the hairs rising on the back of my neck to the uneven beat of my heart. Excitement and adrenaline and trepidation. I don't feel a thirst for knowledge like this with other clients. I never have. But I knew Ella was different from the moment I first laid eyes on her.

Four-count breaths. Four times. Then my mind is clear enough to type in her name. My thumb hovers over the enter key for only a split second.

It's easy.

Too easy.

This is no back-alley hunt through the dark web with exchanges of cryptocurrencies and code words. Every tap of the keys echoes under the sound of the wind against glass. Scroll. Click. Scroll. There are numerous videos to choose from. So many with small thumbnail images of Ella's face. One of her giving the camera the middle finger forces the corners of my lips up. None of them seem too current. All dating from two years ago and further. A tick in the back of my mind notes that it seems some things have been cleared. I'll have to dig deeper for those if there were takedown notices issued.

She has the typical social media platforms. Although I don't dig through those just yet.

Refining the search, and clicking away, I scroll past more photos.

They're all so different from the Ella I know now. The version of a younger, stronger woman in all these thumbnail pictures doesn't have dark smudges under her eyes. Even in the photos, she doesn't appear still and quiet and wounded. I couldn't picture this past-life version of her before, and now that it's in front of me, the change in her is stark and jarring.

A few videos appear in the search, the name of the site flicking on a switch of alarm. Several clicks and my gaze drifts back to her sleeping form, before I go against my better judgment, and follow the link.

More than the pictures, more than the videos themselves, I'm drawn to the comments.

Given that the site has subheadings that include "hardcore," "girl on girl," and "amateur," I'm prepared for some type of deviant evidence to appear. Searching her name, more than twenty videos appear. Each of them displaying her face. Her head is thrown back with pleasure written in her expression. One of her leaning forward in the middle of a bar, her legs spread on the sofa, her attitude playful, yet seductive, and both of her hands wrapped around a champagne bottle, the bubbly spilling down the side. She's clothed in the stills, but I'd be surprised if she remained that way once I clicked on them.

Slipping the headphones into place, I do another check of the monitors, before returning to the site. I have ... specific tastes so I'm not unfamiliar with websites that cater to a certain clientele.

Each video post has hundreds of comments underneath. These are the digital footprints of people who have sat where I'm sitting. They watched these videos in the glow of a hundred different screens, in different sitting rooms and bedrooms and basements.

My body hums with the recognition that this is technically research, but still ... jealousy and possessiveness threaten to piss me off. My skin pebbles with goosebumps and my breathing comes fast and shallow and my hands—

My hands are clenched into fists so tight that my knuckles are white above the keyboards.

It's all because of these fucking comments. Men and women who watched her and discussed it freely. With anxiousness, I shift in my seat, noting each of the videos falls under the category labeled "Exhibitionist."

There's an enormous variety in the types of comments made. Some are completely irrelevant, a simple thumbs-up or emoji. Then there are other, more detailed comments and conversations. Feminist opinions. Misogynistic ones.

And summaries of what happens within the clips.

Summaries—and reactions.

I can't help lingering on those. The first few comments are written in all caps. Ten, twenty exclamation points. They urge the viewers to keep watching. *It gets hotter*, the comments read.

It only takes ten minutes to start recognizing names of the users. Some have returned to the videos again and again, the comments providing that evidence with the dates beside the comments. I recognize two usernames in particular—two men in conversation across multiple videos.

One conversation in particular gives me insight I didn't imagine I'd ever find on a site like this. Dated four years ago.

Where's the one with her on her knees?

Deleted. :(

Fuck me. That was one of my favorites. This one's close, but not the real deal.

It went down with the others when they got engaged. He decides what stays and what goes.

Selfish bastard.

Engaged. Ella was engaged before. A concoction of emotion stronger than whiskey hits me all at once. She was engaged, and from the looks of it, the two of them had a shared proclivity to be watched.

The Dominant side of me shifts in my seat from the uncertainty of their relationship. My preference has always been for discretion when I indulge. The level of discretion displayed in these videos is obviously a different boundary than I have ever committed to.

I almost close the laptop, my mind reeling with more questions than answers, but I stop myself short, one thumbnail calling out to me more than all the others.

The thumbnail is a still of Ella, like the rest, but in this one she wears a bright, innocent smile. When I click through it has the most comments of any of the videos I've searched for in the last half hour.

I can barely focus on them. The first line I read several times, and still the words don't register. I'm not a fool; I know what I'm going to see when I click the play button. Still, I know I shouldn't. And yet, I know I will.

Ella's simper reaches right through the screen to me. Her teeth are sunk into her bottom lips, painted a cherry red as she sits on a man's lap. The man's hand wrapped around her waist splays across her hip. It's a loose hold on her, not at all possessive. The black man smiles, his focus elsewhere as she stares at the camera, a beer held in his right hand. It's not hard to tell that they're at a bar. In public. The mischievousness that glinted in her eyes yesterday morning is there in this photo. Begging me to play.

I have to click play. That's part of the research. Witnessing this is my job. A barely audible voice whispers that it's not my job. That watching these videos—labeled as pornographic in no uncertain terms—could be avoided. No, *should* be avoided.

I don't want to avoid it, though. I'm damn sure of that.

The comments under this particular video are about how it's the beginning. The commenters say it over and over. This is the beginning. This is how it started. How the incident began and to keep watching.

From one of the familiar names, I read the comment, *It's her foreplay.*

I hover my cursor over the video, and it plays a few

seconds in a loop. She's not alone in this three-second clip. Far from alone. I know the place—it's a Hard Rock in Vegas. The background is crowded with patrons coming and going. There's no possibility that anything salacious could happen within this public venue. But whatever did happen, it's clear the other woman in the video was involved.

Because she has her fingertips on Ella's jaw. I'm caught for a long minute watching the three-second clip of her tracing her pale pink painted nails down Ella's jaw, down her neck, and even lower, to where her black-sequined dress barely covers her. The hemline skimming her thighs makes my mouth dry up. Clearing my throat, I check the empty room again. Comforted by silence, I return to the two women.

A hard swallow, watching them, in what I would guess is their midtwenties. The second woman's caramel skin is a few shades darker than Ella's. Her black hair is loosely curled and as Ella leans into her touch, she plays with her friend, or lover's, curls.

The video begins with the other woman, dressed in black leather leggings and a burgundy crop top that shows a sliver of her olive-brown skin, tracing her fingertips over Ella's skin. Over her neck, where I want to touch her. And lower, to where my entire body wishes to be. The two women are standing close to a high-top table, their backs to the crowd. And the way they're looking at each other, the way they're touching—

I scroll back down to the comments. Someone identifies

the woman as Maggie, her friend. The name suits her, with her girl-next-door smile and expressive eyes. The comments are also right that the scene is hot, but it's not just hot.

There's something ... suspenseful about it. The man she was with in the thumbnail watches in the background, his gaze mostly focused on Maggie, but it shifts to Ella as the two women clink cocktail glasses filled with a pink liquid. Over the pounding music, you can barely make out their laughter.

Though they're standing in the bar, it doesn't seem sleazy or even staged, the way most porn on the internet appears. Two women, flirting innocently with each other. Every so often, their eyes go to people outside the frame. I keep the volume down low, really low, but when they speak and I miss what was said, I have to turn it up a notch and then another.

There's not an ounce of shame. And from what I gather on the site, this isn't professional and nothing Ella would be paid for. This isn't her job, it's her life, her wants and desires.

I wonder if she knew it was being filmed. There's no doubt when she stares at the camera, not more than a handful of seconds later, blushing and leaning closer to Maggie to whisper in her ear, all the while keeping her eyes on the camera, that she knows.

A genuine enjoyment shines in her eyes. It sparks in Maggie's too.

"More drinks!" she shouts out of nowhere, downing the beverage in her hand through the thin black straw. The video continues with the two of them dancing, drinking, and Ella finding herself between two men. The front of one whose face is never shown, and the tall, cleanly shaven black man who towers over her. I wonder if he was her fiancé. Although I don't have to wonder for long. Maggie joins them and doesn't hesitate to kiss the man. She calls him Noah. There's a possessiveness but then she holds Ella's gaze, bumping her shoulder into her and the two of them share a sinful look.

And Ella responds to Maggie's touch. Little shivers. Little glances. And those raised eyebrows at someone else behind the camera. The dancing continues and eventually it's the two women again, partying and laughing. For a moment it seems like it was all in good fun and there wasn't a damn thing sordid between any of them. Until they're at the bar and a conversation takes place.

I'm desperate to know what they're saying. A little more volume, and—

"—all play," Ella's saying, to whoever is holding the camera—a phone, I'm assuming. Judging by how the video is in short snippets, and even then, the camera pans and shakes as one would if it were a phone.

I back it up a few seconds.

"We could all play." Ella's grin is a sultry, sparkling thing. "You know I don't mind playing."

A male voice answers her from behind the camera. "Be careful now, kitten." My blood heats at the nickname. *Kitten.*

Maggie's squeal of delight comes with her toppling forward into the frame, a coiled muscular arm wrapping around her waist to keep her steady. "Noah!"

"You better get your girl," jokes a male voice I haven't heard yet. A deep one. If I had to guess, it would be the man from earlier. Answering my guess, he comes into the screen. Noah, Maggie and Ella ... but who's the fourth? I pause, rubbing my eyes and then flicking back through the security cameras.

Is he her fiancé? There's no ring on her finger. My mind races with dates and information I gathered from comments. This must be a video from before. I wonder if Ella isn't the one who uploaded these. I wonder if she doesn't want them available any longer. I wonder, for a moment and then another, if she thinks it was a mistake. But there's no doubt in my mind that if a woman with her wealth didn't want these available, they'd vanish. Just like all media of Ella from the last two years seems to have vanished.

At this point, lines haven't been crossed. I could stop while I'm ahead and read the damn file.

My better judgment tells me not to continue. For my own damn good. With the click of my thumb, I refuse the warning, and watch the scene continue.

Ella pouts subtly, the expression so cute on her lips that it crushes some hidden part of my chest. She shrugs and says, "I'm just having fun."

Maggie's thick curls falling down her front, she rests her head on Ella's shoulder to whisper, "I'm into your kind of fun," and this time, it's Maggie's eyes that find the camera. Biting down on her lower lip, she angles away from the camera, burying her head into Ella's neck.

The scene at the bar continues in short clips. More drinks, more dancing and accidental bumps into one another. The alcohol flows heavily. That's one thing I note the most. They're all drinking, laughing, having a good time.

It's only when the women glance at the camera that anything at all seems provocative.

This video is made up of multiple segments, most of them of Maggie and Ella. Whoever is holding the camera wants their faces and nothing else.

My body temperature rises, and I strip off the long-sleeved shirt I wore tonight. I'd take off the T-shirt underneath if it wouldn't be so obviously unprofessional.

Glancing down at the time, it's only two minutes in when the camera moves to an elevator. Swallowing thickly, I brace myself for what's coming next.

It's inevitable. The four of them together, the girls laughing and teasing the camera. Swingers, maybe? Fuck buddies? I anticipate them kissing in the closed space.

That's what's logically next and surprisingly, I don't want to stop it.

She wants this.

At least in the moment she did. Her dark chestnut gaze is filled with lust as the man behind the camera steps in beside her and the sound of the doors closing accompanies giddy, feminine laughter from Maggie.

It's undeniable that I'm just as worked up in this moment as each of them.

Damn, I want her. I want to reach through the screen and put my hands on her hips. I want to run my thumbs over her jaw and feel that flirtatious smirk. I want to corner her in, a hand on each side of the steel wall behind her and feel the vibrations of her voice when she laughs, which she does often. Again and again in these videos. It's sexy as hell, and taunting—a subtle game they're playing.

It's sexy as fuck. Portraying the act of seduction. If I were there, confined in that space, I'd punish her for it, for allowing everyone to see. I want it all for me.

She'd have to beg me for even considering letting anyone else see that look in her eye, if she were my submissive. I'm rock hard imagining it and contemplating if I would allow it.

With an undertone of something else, something familiar, Ella gets this look in her eyes when she looks at the camera the second the doors close. "James?" She says his name then, almost as if asking permission, or maybe to make sure everything is all right. There's no doubt he's her partner in this. He replies easily and with a tone of approval, "Good girl, kitten."

The phrase brings a glint to her dark eyes, sparking a fire in their depths.

It makes my pulse race. It makes my skin tense. I don't let myself dwell on it for long.

Not that I'm given a chance. The next scene cuts to explicit pornography without any easing into it.

Maggie's slender legs are wrapped around James's waist on the right side of the screen as he thrusts into her. Her eyes are closed in ecstasy and she moans in short staccato cadence in time with the pounding of his hips meeting hers. On the left side of the same bed, Ella is on her knees, her fingers digging into the sheets and Maggie's hand grips hers. Behind Ella, Noah fucks her mercilessly. It's zoomed out, so details are obscure, but not so much that the full picture isn't painted.

"Fuck," Ella breathes into the pillow before biting down on it. Her face is flushed and her full breasts sway with each punishing thrust. Noah's fingers dig into her hips, keeping her exactly where he wants her. A thin lather of sweat glistens from his shoulders. The men's backs are to the camera, leaving the women exposed to the viewer. As Ella's head is thrown back, her gaze meets the lens, and in that moment, she screams out her orgasm.

As much as I want to focus on her, I don't miss how James's concentration moves to Ella in that moment. His gaze stays on her as she calls out her release, balling up the sheets and bringing them closer to her chest. With her head buried in the blankets, Noah races for his own pleasure, fucking her harder and faster.

James takes it as his cue to reposition Maggie, bringing her calves to his shoulder and climbing up higher on the bed until her knees are at her shoulders and her dark eyes go wide. The cords in her neck tighten and she no longer reaches to Ella to hold her hand. Instead, her nails dig into James's back as he eases into her, slowly at first and then deeper, faster, taking Maggie closer to a dangerous edge.

"Yes, yes," Maggie chants between clenched teeth, her pitch getting higher as she fuels James on and he picks up his pace, fucking her relentlessly.

Ella claws across the bed, barely holding on as she writhes under Noah, who slams inside of her, finding his own release.

My cock aches with need at the sight of her drowning in pleasure.

With all of them breathing heavily, lips meet the curves of the women's necks and then their panting slows and small pecks turn deeper. Ella and Maggie got what they wanted. All four of them in one hotel room.

Swapping partners, and once again, they each seek out the camera.

It's porn, what I'm looking at. Homemade porn. No one would call it anything else. I anticipate that being the end but as James stands, it becomes apparent he isn't finished. I size up the man and find him not lacking in both stature and frame. He's classically handsome, dark hair, a clean shave like Noah, preppy even. Toned but not overly muscular. The video captures him pulling off the condom as Noah and Maggie help each other dress. The profile of the two of them kissing blocks my view of Ella, but from the bits that can be seen, she's thrown the covers over herself.

As James's condom falls to a trash can tucked under a desk on the other side of the room, Noah lets out a rough huff of a laugh.

"You cheated," Noah comments from across the room and he's met with a smirk from James. Fully clothed, he nods at a naked James. "You definitely took a V."

James only huffs a laugh before reaching for the phone. Again I expect the video to end, but it doesn't.

"Night, love," James says and the sound of a single kiss is heard. The camera faces a blank wall as they all bid their farewells.

I'm hard as a rock.

Watching her. Watching them. One moment brings my thoughts to a screeching halt. Her ex is leaning over her on the bed. His hand goes to her throat, and Ella takes a breath. One breath. One arch of her back. And I know. I know it for a fact, what she likes, what she wants.

What I could give to her.

And what I can never give to her.

Fuck.

The rustling of the sheets is heard and the camera is positioned face up on a pillow, so all that can be seen is the ceiling.

"Spread your legs for me," James whispers and the camera rocks as James continues to fuck Ella, her sweet moans heard in between sounds of them kissing. It's all audio for the last minute when it finally ends with the camera falling off the bed and hitting the floor.

I watch them again and again. This video. The one from the bar. Every other video in the set. They span a seven-year period with nearly half of them from the first two years. Then only a video a year, some with two. The bar scene is the last one. Not all of them feature her ex, but he's there in some capacity for most of them. The night turns to a deep black, black as my soul must be from watching this and confirming my suspicions. The autumn fire of dawn catches in slow increments as I watch and watch and watch.

Once it's over, I click back to the cameras, flicking through the videos of nothing. Not a damn thing has changed, yet it feels like everything has.

"Hey."

Damon's voice scares the living shit out of me, but I control it. I control the startle reflex and the wild hum of my pulse and nod at his silhouette from across the room in the morning light. Rubbing my hands over my face, I play it off as exhaustion. I close the laptop gently as if I've been doing the kind of research that involves files and records and interviews. "Hey." If I were a better man, I'd feel any sort of shame, but at the moment, I don't.

"She still sleeping?" he asks.

"I haven't heard any movement."

He nods. "You're good to go."

I don't wait a second to get the hell out of that room. I want to stay too badly to wait. More than anything, I want to take the steps up to Ella's bedroom two at a time and show her I understand, at least a little more. I understand the part of her who could use attention that I could give her. At least for a little while. Not forever, because nobody wants a fucked-up prick like me forever. But I could satisfy a part of her that shares reciprocal needs and give us both a much-needed distraction.

CHAPTER 8

ELLA

*A partner of The Firm will immediately respond to a
client's distress signals by providing one-on-one support.
This may include a counseling session, medical attention,
or an otherwise agreed-upon mediation.*

T oday is not a good day. There are good days and there
are bad days. "Bad" isn't a strong enough word for how
fucking awful they are, but I suppose it's the appropriate
counter to good.

The moment I woke up, I knew every minute was going
to be harder than the last. The moment my eyes opened and
I forgot, then remembered ... that was my warning. It's an
emptiness that takes over initially. It seeps slowly within me

throughout the day, making the tips of my fingers cold at first and then it spreads. My mouth turns dry, my stomach empty but I don't wish to fill it. I don't want to be warm, I don't want my thirst quenched. The only desire is to sit in it, to feel that desolation so as to ensure I won't forget again. Because how could I have possibly forgotten? How could I not wake up every day and feel that loss?

Tears prick at the back of my already tired eyes and like always, I ignore them. I don't allow anything to fall. I've never been a fan of crying. Not since I was a little girl and the videos of me mourning my mother being taken from me, her subsequent suicide, and my father's treatment toward me ... it all led to useless tears and each video I'd made was played back until I realized how much I truly hated the act of crying. So if I can, I withhold it; I acknowledge the urge, but I don't like to see the tears fall.

Instead, I blow across the steam of the fifth cup of tea I've made today. I thought Damon may have been able to smell the whiskey remnants in the last cup. I thought when he left after he offered to pick up for me and refill it, that he would go check the surveillance feed and discover I'd spiked the drink.

I've never held my breath over the judgment of a man I'm not sleeping with, but I'd be damned if I said I didn't then. All day, he's given me space, allowed me to simply lie here, the television screen on, yet with only a logo blinking across it since I haven't pressed play for hours.

Kam slipped me an apology package a couple days ago after our blowup, six little glass bottles of amber warmth. It's an expensive variety and they fit neatly in the small pocket of my robe. I've gone through three so far today. Well, two and a half. The rest of the previous bottle is tucked away beneath the throw pillow under my arm. I hid it there just in case Damon came back with accusations rather than a fresh cup.

Luckily for me, Damon doesn't suspect anything. If he does, he allows me to have it without mentioning it. Every day, I trust him more. I told him so just yesterday and before he left, he told me every day he trusted me more too. It would be horrid of me to break that trust the very next day.

The thought hovers at the back of my mind as I blow across the tea, feeling the billow of steam tickle the tip of my nose.

I don't sip; it's far too hot as it is. The ceramic clinks as I set it down on the mahogany coffee table and lay back into the tan tweed sofa. The walls of the rec room are an off-white hue and if I truly wished to drift off to sleep, I know I would have emptied that little glass bottle just like Alice did on her way to Wonderland. I also would have chosen the much darker sitting room, or the guest bedroom with its thick velvet curtains.

Choosing the rec room, choosing to prop my head up on the pillow rather than bury my face into the cushion, choosing to turn on the television, although I have amazingly failed at such a simple task of watching a mundane home improvement show that I would have devoured years ago—all of that—proves I'm fighting sleep. The steam drifts from the teacup and I watch it dissipate in the dim light from the sconce on the far wall.

There's a soft creak of the floorboards behind the entryway and I nearly give in to the instinct to look, but I refuse it. If I make eye contact with Damon or someone else, they'll ask me questions.

"Do you need anything?" "What is it you want?" "Can I do something to help?"

Every question adds a weight to my chest. I don't have answers for myself, let alone anyone else. Especially right now, when I'm having trouble fighting back my demons.

Let me be. Let them swallow me whole. Why should they concern themselves with the devil of a hell only I'm invited to?

"There you are." The rough timbre from behind me is soothing as it caresses every inch of me. I hear him, I feel him; his presence overwhelms me before I even open my eyes.

I don't want him now, though. Not like this. Not when I'm barely holding on.

My eyes are barely open as I watch him, remaining completely still where I am sprawled across the sofa. I'm aware my robe is open slightly, the delicate silk so easily parted. Beneath it is what I wore to bed last night, a simple chiffon chemise.

I anticipate the questions. At the very least, some variation of, "How are you today?" And when they don't come, some insecurity I'm not at all comfortable with wonders if he'll chastise me for my attire. Of all the things in the world, that sneaks to the surface. My father's scolds reverberate in the back of my skull, springing up from the depths I'd pushed them to decades ago.

My gaze shifts from the hem of my nightgown, where apparently shame resides, to a dark gray fleece blanket that's gently placed over my body.

With my lips parted in protest, I meet Zander's gaze and I'm silenced by it. The intensity. The ownership.

It steals everything from me.

"You'll be cold without it," is the only explanation he offers me. As he steps away from the sofa, I wish I had the courage to tell him I'm cold with it as well, but I'm silent.

He's donned a faded pair of jeans he wears often, I absently wonder if they're his favorite, and a white, long-sleeved polo. Simple yet still seemingly refined on a rugged man like him. Especially when paired with his five o'clock shadow.

The moment I prepare to ask for privacy, already feeling the disappointment growing in my chest, Zander stands, leaving the long chair on the side of the room and instead taking a seat at the end of the sofa I'm occupying. The sofa groans, the sound swallowing the protest that's caught at the back of my throat. He's so very close, I nearly have to bend my legs even further so my feet won't be in the way. As it is, I don't have to, nor do I dare move at all.

Although I do have the urge to stretch out my legs and place my feet in his lap. I resist it successfully, though, waiting instead for Zander to speak.

I haven't wanted to see anyone else, let alone talk all morning and evening, but right now the only thing screaming to be heard from my lips is *speak*.

I want an explanation. The men typically stay several feet away, but Zander seems to have forgotten that. He stretches out casually, although his stiffness tells me he's anything but.

Leaning back, he exhales in an exaggerated huff and then peers down at me.

I don't have the willpower for silence any longer, so I ask the first thing that comes to mind, "Did you give in to curiosity and read my file?"

"Almost ..." he admits and my stomach churns. I used to pride myself on how few fucks I gave over anyone's opinion. Right now, though, it's as if we're surrounded by these fucks like wildflowers in a field. Flowers that could be easily plucked if only he wanted.

"Can you promise me something?" I question and then clear my throat, taking a moment to sip the now lukewarm tea.

"Depends on what it is."

"Don't read it." I speak without daring to look at him.

"Don't read the file, or don't look into your past?"

"Both?" I say, with more hope in my tone than I'd like.

"What if I already know some things?"

I fret under his scrutiny, and place the teacup back down on the table rather than answering.

"I promise I won't read the file, and I'll come to you if I have questions about … well, you."

"No FBI digging?"

"Does the FBI have a file too?"

"Not that I'm aware of."   Although my comment is dry, Zander laughs. It's that genuine, rough laugh that's deep and soothing in ways it shouldn't be.

I chew on the inside of my cheek to keep from asking him what he knows. Shifting under the blanket, I realize how cold I was before. It's already warmer, already promising me sleep.

After a moment of only silence, Zander says, "I could read, or I could talk … Or I could listen."

"I'd rather not talk today."

"Mmm," he hums in a deep rumble, "and of course today was the day I chose to bombard you with questions."

I give him a small laugh, part of it genuine.

"You have questions, don't you? Questions for me?" he asks and the opening he's given me grabs my attention.

"You and Cade are brothers?"

"That's an easy one. And yes, we are."

"You look alike but your last name is what gave it away."

"That'll do it," he comments.

"Have you always been close?"

His brow pinches and he quickly exhales. "No. Not at all."

I don't have to pry further. He freely offers me his story, which includes another brother I didn't know about—William.

"He was six years older than me and from that alone you'd think he'd have been the responsible one. There was him, then Cade and then three years later, me, the baby brother."

It's hard to imagine a man like Zander as the baby.

"Our mom passed away while I was a freshman in college. Our dad had cancer and Cade and William were arguing over a few things."

"I'm so sorry," I tell him and his hand falls onto my calf where he gives me a gentle squeeze. The blanket separates us, but still, his touch ignites me. It doesn't seem to bother him in the least. As if touching me were the natural thing to do.

His swallow is audible and when he doesn't continue, instead staring ahead at the same logo flitting across the television that's kept me company for hours, I nearly push for more, but I don't have to. He leans forward with a huff, grabbing the remote and turning the TV off altogether while telling me the rest of it.

"William wanted my father to live with him during chemo treatments. Cade refused to let it happen. William owed him money and had a gambling addiction. He accused William of trying to take our father's income."

Shock widens my eyes. "That ... couldn't have gone over well."

Shaking his head, Zander agrees. "They were fighting on the front porch, screaming at each other. I jumped in the middle of it to tell them both off. The three of us were yelling like crazy and that's when my father got pissed off and told us all to go home." Zander licks his lower lip, then offers me a sad smile. "He died later that night."

The tears prick again, but I can't hold them back this time. "I'm so sorry," I tell him and wipe under my eyes.

"It happened eight years ago now. But I didn't speak to either of my brothers for years after, other than the occasional text on holidays and birthdays. We were close. Then one day … we weren't."

"What changed?"

"I went through some things two years ago and Cade was there."

"What about William?"

"I was never close with William. He and Cade have their history, but it's the same with William as it's always been. I hear from him when he needs something."

"I'm sorry to hear that."

"You're awfully sorry for me tonight," Zander says as if it's a joke. "Want to know the dirt on Cade from when we were in high school?" he offers with a smirk. "You can't tell him I told you, though."

"You're awful," I say and gently brush my foot against his thigh as if it's an admonishment, although a smile is clearly seen on my face. "And of course I do. Spill it."

The next stories are far more entertaining, although I find myself comparing his childhood experiences to mine. His are ... so much more innocent than my own. Even with things like sneaking out at night and replacing his father's bourbon with colored water being his examples of why they were bad children, they weren't at all compared to the horrific shit I got into. My father was long gone by then, though. If Kam hadn't been there for me, I'd have gone off the deep end ages ago.

I don't tell Zander that. I simply listen to his tales as if they were sweet lullabies. The soothing cadence of his deep voice distracts me from my previous plans.

Time slips by much faster than it did before.

My eyes are heavy as my head sinks deeply into the soft down feather pillow. As I shrug my shoulder in an attempt to pull the soft fleece higher, Zander aids me, tugging the blanket up and tucking it under my chin.

With a simper gracing my lips, I peek up at him and he offers me the kind of smile that threatens to break me. A kind one. Sincere and hopeful.

My own vanishes and I close my eyes tighter, feigning exhaustion as I rub my eyes and destroy his efforts to keep the blanket tucked over me securely. I nearly ask him to go, but I don't. As the tears come, I pull the blanket up higher, hiding and wanting to bury myself in it. Maybe I'll regret it, but right now, I'd regret not leaning into him more than anything if I don't do it this second.

I crawl closer to him, turning around so I'm able to push my body into his. His left arm raises, giving me room and I put the pillow on his thigh. At least I give him that to separate us. My breathing struggles as I bury my head there, pretending the dams haven't broken. His arm lays easily against my body, the weight of it hugging my curves. His warmth is instant. He doesn't shush me, but he does hum lightly; it's a soothing rumble.

The overwhelming sadness came from nothing and it feels like everything. I swear I was okay. I was.

With heat rising to my face as tears pool under my eyes, I focus on his strong hand splayed over my hip, his thumb rubbing soothing motions.

The sobs take over; I can't control them. I wish I could hide my face better, but Zander refuses to let me, brushing the hair out of my face. In an attempt to swat away his hand so I can hide beneath my dark locks, I lift my arm, but his grip is faster. Catching my wrist in his hand.

Inhaling deeply, I peer up at him through my thick lashes, tainted with beads of tears. My vision is still blurry when the rough pad of his thumb runs under my eyes. One at a time, ever so gently, and at odds with the calluses he's earned over the years.

The distraction pulls me from my outburst and a moment passes and then another before my breathing has steadied again, and I'm able to fully recollect what happened.

Neither of us speaks for a long moment as I calm myself, taking in long inhales and blowing out even longer exhales.

He's the first to speak and although I dread it, I'm grateful he takes the lead in the conversation.

"Do you know what brought it on?" he questions me just as I'm replaying the scene in my mind. Shaking my head I whisper no and consider moving, but he's still running those soothing circles through the thin fabric of my nightgown. More importantly, the pillow shifted at some point behind me, and now my cheek rests firmly against his thigh. The jeans aren't nearly as comfortable pressed against my skin, but they smell like him.

And he's so damn warm. Everything about him is comforting. Almost familiar in some strange way.

"I don't know," I add and note that my throat feels like it's on fire. I barely even spoke today. Just as I'm reaching up to my throat, Zander reaches across me, one hand holding me in place, the other picking up the cup and handing it to me.

"Drink and tell me if you need it warm," he commands. I obey, the peppermint soothing even though the tea is now cold.

"Sometimes it'll come from nowhere," he says as if justifying my outburst but then he adds, "Are you familiar with the 'ball in a box' analogy?"

I shake my head, never having heard of it. He explains,

"The ball is large, filling the box when grief first appears. There's a small button on one side of the box but the ball is so big it constantly bumps against it, triggering the emotional response. As time goes on, the ball shrinks in size, moving and colliding into the walls and occasionally, the button. There's no stopping it and no matter how small the ball gets, there's always a chance it will hit the button. There's no preventing it."

"I think my ball might be very big," is all I can comment.

Zander nods and says, "There's nothing wrong with that."

A long moment passes of comfortable silence before Zander seems to take note of our proximity.

"You're tired—"

Before he's even said it, I know he's going to tell me I need to go to bed. So I cut him off and say, "I don't want to sleep."

A moment passes, with the click of the heater coming on ensuring we're both aware of just how silent it is between us. For the second time tonight, I feel insecure wondering what his response will be. Whether he'll respect my desire to stay up or not. Or if he'll push me to go to bed. "Please don't make me," I plead with him in a whisper. It's a foolish request.

"I won't ever make you do anything you don't want to. Unless it's for your own good."

I raise a brow in question, unable to help myself from saying, "And sleeping in bed?"

Staring at me, he takes a moment longer before ignoring

my question altogether and asking me, "I just remembered another time Cade got in trouble and blamed it on me. Do you want to hear it?"

There's a pull at the corners of my lips and I nod before lying back down where I was, pulling the gray fleece up and setting the pillow back down. I'm more than aware of how inappropriate it is, and how little I care.

And this is how I drift off to sleep. Listening to stories told in the soothing cadence of a man I consider confessing all my stories to.

CHAPTER 9

ZANDER

Partners of The Firm will maintain appropriate
professional conduct with clients at all times.

Ella drifts to sleep on my lap.

But I've never been more awake in my life. I couldn't
sleep if I wanted to. I keep talking long after she's out,
until my throat goes so dry I can't say another word. Every
heartbeat feels like an electric shock. What we're doing is
technically within the bounds of her contract with The Firm.
That's what I tell myself, at least. Professional conduct can
include physical touch. It's impossible to avoid sometimes
when you're providing security for a client. You take their
arm and shield them from prying eyes as they exit a vehicle,

or a building. You tuck them into your side when moving through an unruly crowd.

My hands have been on both male and female clients before. Not once has it been an issue. Not once has it been ... like *this*.

There are provisions for physical touch in Ella's contract too. I know there are. I know because we had a team meeting about it when Cade pitched the case to the rest of us. There was no way around it. We're here twenty-four hours a day and we are required, *required*, to provide emotional support.

But this ...

Does not feel like providing emotional support.

It feels like knocking down brick walls with a sledgehammer, for the both of us. Her walls are obvious and where my attention should be, yet I can't help but to notice my own. The one I've kept in place for years now. It feels like giving something to myself just as much as it feels like giving something to her.

There aren't any provisions for that in the contract. I don't get anything out of this but a salary. That's the rule, and them's the breaks.

Too fucking bad.

I stretch out my free arm—the one not running softly up and down the bare skin exposed by the sleeve of Ella's robe riding up slightly. My hand splays out under the throw pillow on the sofa in my effort to stretch.

And meets glass.

A tiny glass bottle.

I pull it out and examine it in the light. It's one of those miniature bottles of alcohol.

Are you fucking kidding me? The disbelief is as palpable as the discontent.

No wonder she looked like she was going to pass out. She'd been drinking. Not much, given the size of the bottle, and it shouldn't react badly with the meds she's on. Assuming she only had one.

But she shouldn't be drinking at all. We were supposed to clear the house of all alcohol before she moved in. I thought we'd gotten rid of it all. *How the hell did this get past Damon?*

Irritation wars with concern inside of me. This could have gone so very wrong.

Ella's shoulders rise and fall with a whimper, almost as if she can feel my disappointment with her. And there's that wall again, destroyed and leaving me wanting nothing more than to refuse any backsteps after the moment I had with her tonight.

My thumbnail taps against the glass and I know it's something to look into, but not something I can do a damn thing about right now.

It's a problem for later. After deciding what to do about the matter, I tuck the bottle back under the pillow.

"Ella."

She doesn't wake. Doesn't so much as stir. Her breathing has gone slow and even. I imagine she needs a deep sleep, but even so I monitor her breathing and when she stirs, fighting the urge to wake up, I let her fall back under, rather than rousing her to consciousness.

She can't sleep here. I'm quiet as I stand, preparing to take her upstairs and put her in her bed. The idea of putting her to bed is met with thoughts that shouldn't be anywhere on my mind. Specifically: reddening her ass with my itching palm for hiding alcohol.

Even that small thought has my cock hardening.

Fuck.

Calm focus. Four-count breaths. Four times over. There are eyes everywhere in this house. Cameras. Every move I make needs to be carefully considered, because even if I alter some of the footage, there can be nothing suspicious about the rest, nothing to indicate that my heart is beating out of my chest and I want to kiss her awake. Run roughshod over her boundaries. And punish her ass so she won't sneak alcohol again.

So damn badly.

More than I've wanted anything since Quincy.

But I don't kiss her. I'm a goddamn professional, and I don't kiss her. I maneuver Ella into my arms in a chaste carry, her warm body curled against my chest. Her head rests easily against my shoulder. She's so deeply asleep I have to cradle her tighter than I otherwise would. Far tighter than would be considered professional.

The herringbone stairs leading up to the second floor are dark, but I trust them to be empty in this barren, spotless house. They are. A nightlight in the upstairs hall casts enough of a glow for me to see that Ella's bedroom door is ajar. I nudge it open the rest of the way with my shoulder and carry her to the bed.

This part takes more planning. I don't think she'll stand, so I keep her in my arms and nudge the covers down as best I can, then lower her to the sheets.

Ella's almost there when she startles, a tiny jerk of her body against mine. Her arms come up and around my neck and holy shit, she can hold tight. Her grip is solid and strong and her forehead presses into the side of my neck, her breath warm on my skin. I feel that all the way down to my erection. It only takes a moment for her to loosen her grasp, falling back into a deep sleep.

I take a ragged breath and force myself to it again. She is sleeping. She's not aware of what she's doing, let alone what she does to me. I move to lower her the rest of the way, but even when Ella's body makes contact with the mattress, she doesn't let go completely.

"Sleep with me," she murmurs, her voice tactile on my skin. "Zander. Stay."

My name. Her lips. That voice.

Fuck.

It takes more strength than I would have thought to untwist her arms from my neck. "It's time for you to sleep." I use my professional voice now, firm but not cold. Ella won't remember that I've also used a touch of my Dominant side. She shivers beneath me.

Maybe she will remember.

She turns over and slips one wrist under her pillow. I feel like a monster standing over her like this. Wanting her like this. Wanting, with every last bit of my soul, to crawl into bed next to her and sleep and sleep and sleep.

Then wake to do other things.

It's torture to stay and wait for her breathing to even out.

Ella rolls over again, her eyes catching the faint light. "Please?" The word is a breath on her lips that must contain witchery. It's potent enough to cast spells.

I put a hand out and stroke her hair. This is allowed. This is a professional touch between a client and a member of The Firm. This is to provide her with the emotional support she's desperate for. Calmly I give her the command, "Sleep."

"Sleepless dreams," she murmurs and closes her eyes.

Dreamless sleep. That's what she means. I have dreamless nights now, thanks to the little blue pills, but I know what happens when I go off them. I know what I'll see when I close my eyes for the night. Memories rush in and try to fill the room. I push them away one by one. We're not doing this tonight. I am on the clock.

A few minutes of soft breathing, and Ella rolls over onto her back.

It takes everything I have, every ounce of self-control, to do what I have to do next.

I flip up her nightgown. Not so far that it uncovers the soft flesh of her belly—just far enough to access the belt to the robe. I can't leave her to sleep tangled in the silk garment. I've watched her in bed before. I know exactly how she sleeps, although stripping her down entirely is out of the question.

Touching her as little as possible, I maneuver the robe from her shoulders, sliding it down without disturbing her. Ella is so warm. So soft. Everything I want to do to her strikes me as I focus on simply removing the robe. My hands ache with the urge to touch her and feel exactly how soft she is. I want to skim my hands up under her nightgown to her tits. I want to drag a fingertip around each nipple until it pebbles for me.

I want to put my hand around her throat. Not to constrict her breathing, just enough for her to feel it. No. I only want to hold her in my grip. It would be good for her. Maybe that's the assessment of a broken man who is searching for excuses, but I think it would. Here in the dark, in her bedroom, I think it would be good for her. It would give her a sense of safety. If she can't be in control, then I'll be in control for her.

I bow my head instead of shaking it and ease the robe

over her hips, down her thighs, all the way to her ankles.

And then I pull it off.

I watch her a moment longer, ignoring every sordid thought I have, and then I leave, closing the door behind me. I leave her in her bedroom, with all its pristine shelves and empty surfaces. There's practically nothing in there. Sparse as a hotel room. Ella is the room's most interesting feature.

My heart beats hard with new adrenaline. My shift isn't over, and my to-do list isn't finished. In the rec room I sit down on the couch and slide my hand under the pillow. The little bottle of alcohol is half-empty. This can't have been the only one, can it? She didn't smuggle in a single-serving shot.

There were probably more.

If I want to find out, I'm going to have to ask Damon. We work two days on, two days off. Silas and Dane take the days in between. Damon works the day shift on our days and there's no doubt in my mind that she drank at least half this bottle today while he was here.

For a split second, I wonder if I should inform him at all. Partly to protect her from his future precautions, but also because I'd much rather punish her myself. Without prying eyes and paperwork.

The glass bottle stares back at me.

Do I throw this thing out or leave it where it is?

I think of Ella's pale face. The way she crawled toward me. The hundred other small things she did that beg for protection. That beg for a second chance. I'm not going to fuck this up for her. A powerful urge makes me stand up from the couch. I need to protect her.

I picture her here, facing off with Cade as he questions her about the bottle and how she got it and if she has more alcohol. He'd insist on a session with her and the Rockford Center professionals. Her cheeks would flush, and her eyes would dart to mine, and I wouldn't be able to stop myself. I wouldn't be able to deny her an escape, even if this is what I'm being paid to do.

Fuck. Fuck.

Taking long, deliberate strides, I go into the kitchen and throw it out. Bury it deep in the trash can. We've cleared the house, so no one is checking the garbage. And no one will check this time. The deceit burrows into my chest and throbs there like a kind of infection, but what the hell else am I supposed to do?

My options are to call for backup, document this transgression, or take care of it myself.

I'm choosing door number three.

Four-count breaths. Four of them. If the situation worsens, I will follow protocol. But tonight I'm going to allow her this one thing. This one last barrier between Ella and the world we've created for her. I'll gift her this secret.

Which means ...

Back in the rec room, I open my laptop. It hums to life,

the keys cool under my fingers. It's been off for most of my shift, but it boots up immediately like it's been waiting for me. In a way, it has.

I go into the program that manages the security cameras. It takes a surprisingly small number of clicks to erase the two hours of footage. That footage includes our conversation, me finding the bottle for the first time, and me carrying Ella upstairs in my arms.

Guilt tightens my throat. I don't know what to feel more guilty about—doing my job in an unorthodox way, or the things I'm feeling for the woman sleeping upstairs. It's a storm of guilt. It's an old wound ripped open, over and over again.

When the files are gone, I check the feeds.

Ella sleeps peacefully in her room.

There's no other movement in the house. Damon won't be here for several hours.

Which gives me plenty of time for more research. No matter what I said to Damon, I won't be reading that file. Especially not now when I promised her I wouldn't. The drinking ... however, is something I had already noticed from the videos the other night. There might be evidence of a substance abuse problem. It wouldn't be shocking. She wouldn't be the first person in the world to self-medicate.

The initial search turns up nothing. Not even a hint. Nothing indicating the existence of any sealed files.

Searching takes up most of the space in my mind. I don't

take my mind off of Ella completely—that would be reckless, and a dereliction of duty. But I do allow myself a calm focus on the search. I ignore my aching cock and my pounding heart and keep typing different phrases and terms, all of them paired with Ella's name.

When nothing comes, I research my options with her. The therapy I once had and the steps I took back then compared to what's available to me now.

All the while, she sleeps. If she dreams, I hope it's of me.

"Morning."

I curse under my breath but manage not to reach for the laptop. "Make a little noise coming in, would you?" I look up into Damon's face, intending to make this a joke.

His usual smile is gone. His expression is dead serious, and his dark eyes travel over me on the couch and my laptop sitting in front of me. "Everything go all right last night?"

"Yes." Now I do reach for the computer and close the top with as much casual indifference as I can muster. "Ella's still sleeping. She slept most of the night after we had a brief conversation. I don't have any other notes."

"You sure it went all right?" Damon's brow furrows a little. He doesn't hide the suspicion in his gaze.

For a moment, I think of telling him. I could open my mouth and do it right now. I could say I was supposed to be giving her emotional support, and I didn't cross any lines. Except in my own goddamn head.

Damon, of all people, would understand. Hell, he's even kept secrets for me in the past. But telling anyone is a risk I'm not willing to take.

"I'm sure," I tell him. "It was an uneventful night."

CHAPTER 10

ELLA

Any and all crucial information pertaining to the state of the client must be provided without hesitation to all partners of The Firm by the client or custodial guardian. It is critical that any source of threat or trigger is identified so as to establish a safe space for the client.

It feels as if I've slept more last night than I have in a year. And I didn't take a pretty little blue pill to ensure those hours of sleep. It's the afternoon by the time I finally wake. Although I do so with a migraine that pounds at my temples. It happens sometimes, after a hard night of crying. Yet another reason I despise tears.

Shuffling to the bathroom, I take my time taking two

Advil, washing my face, brushing my teeth, combing my hair. All the while last night plays back in my mind as if it were a dream.

It's not until I step out of the bathroom and find my robe folded in half that I register not remembering coming to bed. The image of Zander, laying me down in bed, ignites far too much heat for what it was.

The racing of my heart is also unjustified, since I know it will be Damon downstairs waiting for me, not the man I dreamed about last night.

"What are these?" My brow pinches as my black ballerina house slippers tap on the porcelain floor. Three notebooks lay at my spot at the kitchen island. Damon is always on the left side with me at the right when I start my day. We've developed a sort of routine. And at my spot, piled on top of one another, are three thick binders and a cup filled with colored pens and highlighters. Inhaling a steadying breath, I peer across the island and dare him to tell me he expects me to start coloring my doodles.

Damon's attire is business casual, which is at complete odds with the silk camisole and matching tap pants I slipped on. The only commonality is that we're both wearing black. It's a suitable color as I mourn the state of my headache.

It would be almost comical to compare the two of us. This man exudes strength. I think he could make the cheapest of clothes look expensive. There's even a hint of danger in his deep brown eyes, and a charming smile. The cadence of his voice is far too soothing for a man who could do so much damage.

I'm certain he's broken more than a few hearts in his lifetime. My gaze shifts down to his fingers currently wrapped around the handle of a coffee mug, and I note the distinct lack of a wedding ring. He has most certainly left a trail of broken hearts in his wake over the past decade.

"We don't want to rush anything," Damon starts, "but I thought you might like one of these better."

He gestures to the stack of journals and continues with his normal daytime push for me to consider jotting down any thoughts or feelings that I'd rather not share out loud. Which would be any thoughts or feelings at all. So far, I've only managed to sketch a bit and even that took its toll a time or two.

The first is a deep red and I'm quick to toss it to the side. Damon jokes, which he never does, teasing "next," and forcing a small smile to my lips.

The second has tiny boxes rather than lines in the interior. It reminds me of graphing paper and I'm not a fan of it at all.

The last one is soft leather and my fingertips can't help trailing down the rose gold binding. The leather itself is a pale white, although the pages inside are thick and heavy, and have a tinge of burgundyish, pale pink to them. It's incredibly feminine and the very idea that this man bought it personally ... well again I find myself smiling this afternoon with a bit of humor.

"We have a winner?" he asks and I nod, giving in to the acceptance of a new journal but not promising to write anything just yet.

"Can I make you anything to eat?"

Answering him with a "no, thank you," the sputtering at the coffee machine hits me just then. As does the scent of, I think, waffles. From the corner of the island, maple syrup is visible as well as the butter dish.

"Are you finally taking my suggestion to eat here?"

Damon busies himself with his cup of coffee and glances over his shoulder, then says, "You could say that." I'm not sure why, but that makes me smile too.

Getting myself comfortable, I shift up onto the stool. My slippers fall off one at a time, thudding onto the floor. My bare toes rest against the metal bar of the stool. With my elbow on the island and my chin resting in my hand, I wonder more about this man and his relationship with Zander.

"I really like this one," I comment, tapping the soft leather.

"Good." Damon's gaze moves to the journal in question. "If I make you a cup of tea, will you write something today?"

A small laugh bubbles at my lips, and even through my headache that's beginning to wane, I feel a sense of ease. "Is that not coercion?"

Damon's rough chuckle only reminds me that last night

I heard Zander laugh, only sort of like that. It was deeper, it was smoother ... it's a sound I'd like to hear again.

It's typical for Damon to urge me to open up first thing on the days he's here. Maybe he knows I'm most vulnerable then, when I'm tired and still waking up. I've never been a morning person. He says whatever he can to start conversation, occasionally asking me mundane questions and a piece of me wants to take him up on this offer and ask him more about Zander. At the same time, that's not the game that we're playing. For some odd reason, it also feels like a betrayal.

As Damon builds his case for a cup of tea being a worthy exchange for a page of thoughts, anything at all, I meander to the stack of waffles and make myself a plate.

I like Damon as much as I like Silas and Dane. They are protective, they give me space when I ask for it, they don't judge me like so many others have throughout my entire life. But I don't dream of them at night.

Flutters rise when I remember last night, and how I rested my head in Zander's lap. Shivers threaten at the memory of his hand slipping down my hip.

"What do you say?" Damon questions with a raised brow, raising a glass mug with one hand, tea bag held in the other.

I take him up on his offer, if only to please him so that when I have the courage to ask about Zander, he'll share with me. A little give, a little take.

And so I spend my brief day with Damon ridding myself

of a migraine brought on by the hard sobs of last night, but playing out the events without any remorse or regret. With a heavy yet slim pen dancing between my fingers, the ink flowing across the thick pages of the new journal, I daydream of him, but write stories of my childhood. Of what I know I missed, having to grow up so young. But also what I wish I could take back.

I'm far too close to the fireplace. Its dancing blue flames mesmerize me to the point where I haven't realized how warm I am until the deep voice speaks from behind me.

"Damon said you have a new journal."

Even the physical heat surrounding me pales in comparison to what he does to me. Every inch of me is too hot when I lay eyes on him. More than likely it's because his gaze rests on me.

"Did you write anything down today?"

How can he ask something so uninteresting when all I can imagine is picking up where we left off last night, with our hands searching for something to hold us steady and daring to lift my lips to his?

Lying on the hard herringbone floor with a pool of fabric at my feet and two of the cushions from the sofa, one for my head and the other supporting my shoulder, I prop myself up off the floor to stare up at him.

Zander towers over me, a dominating air surrounding him that's only shown whispers of itself before.

"I wrote a few things." I answer him out of respect once the weight of what he's asked me sinks in fully. "I'd rather not talk about it."

Zander takes a step forward, his jeans rustling and when he takes a place next to me on the floor, I notice he's taken his shoes off. His bare feet match the untamed man he is. Sitting cross-legged, and wearing a dark gray Henley, everything feels different between us. There's no melody to dance to any longer. No notes to hide behind. I search his hazel eyes and find the fire dancing in the reflection.

"You don't want to talk about what you wrote? Or you don't want to talk about anything?" he questions so casually with an innocent expression on his handsome face, one would think his inquiry didn't carry the weight of the world with it. The soothing crackle of the fire is the only distraction between us when I scoot forward and readjust some, sitting on my ass with my feet planted on the floor and bringing my knees into my chest.

"I think I could talk today, I just have boundaries."

"Boundaries?" Zander repeats the single word and somehow it sounds sinful on his lips. All the tension evaporates, leaving behind a magnetic pull that I can't resist. "We could discuss boundaries." If I'm not mistaken, at his lips is the hint of a smirk, but he holds it back. "Is that what you want to talk about today? Boundaries?"

I search his expression for the answer to my unspoken

thought: *What type of boundaries are you referring to?*

The devilish smirk he'd been trying to hide breaks through. And I find myself wearing a matching simper.

As I rise from the floor, eager to get away from the fire and what is now nearly stifling heat, I contemplate teasing him. Calling him out for the fact that this feels very much like flirting and significantly less like counseling. Just as the words are ready to slip from my lips, Zander stands alongside me, his right hand taking mine and his left bracing my elbow to help me rise.

I've had many social interactions, and I've learned a few important details about seemingly innocent touches. When a person makes contact with you, whether a hand on an elbow or a friendly hug, the longer the contact lingers, the more they want to fuck you. A quick hug and a hand releasing into the air once the connection begins to break, rather than slipping down the small of your back, is very good evidence there's no sexual chemistry.

Which is not at all what happens right now.

The way Zander trails his fingertips along my forearm and then down my torso, splaying his hand against the small of my back as I stand, tells me everything I want to know. My wild heart beats rapidly. I'm not sure if it's in protest, or if it's simply come back to life, but for a moment, I'm caught. Trapped and unable to think of anything other than my heart's existence.

Concern mars Zander's face as he peers down at me, and I struggle to remember what we were even talking about. "Did I already take it too far?"

"Not at all." My lower lip slips between my teeth as I struggle with whether or not I should add, *I don't believe you've gone far enough.* I keep the thought to myself and turn my back to him to make my way to the sofa. "I just thought we should be comfortable for our session."

There's an undeniable electricity between the two of us. Again, I'm reminded of that dance I felt the first morning that we were alone together. I take one corner of the sofa, and Zander chooses a chair across the room, the one farthest away.

"I think we should start with confessions," Zander begins.

"I've never been a fan of confessions," I say, then nearly continue with a phrase that I've said a number of times in my life: "Confessions imply regret. I live my life with no regrets whatsoever." But then I remember. I remember it all and every regret threatens to suffocate me until Zander tells me, "I've seen some videos and I have questions."

"That's your confession, that you've seen videos?"

A nagging thought pricks at the back of my mind. It was only last night I asked him not to look up any information on me, but the slight feeling of betrayal is quickly pacified.

"It was before last night," he says, and vulnerability shines in his eyes. "I want to make sure you know that." The relief is met with cautiousness. He didn't tell me he knew before, but it's obvious that he feels remorse.

The sofa protests as I pull my legs up, resting the balls of my feet on the cushion and leaning back into the pillow. "I appreciate you telling me." The kindness between us doesn't diminish the chemistry. Although I attempt a more casual stance by resting my head on the arm of the sofa, Zander remains professional.

"I want you to know that I meant it when I said I won't look at your file, but I am damn curious and I'd like to speak freely with you."

"Regarding those videos?" There's a hint of a tease there, but also a sadness.

"More than just the videos. You ... captivate me."

His confession only adds to my own curiosity about what this man wants from me. About what he could do to me. The nervousness is evident in the tapping of his thumb on the armrest.

"What did you think?" I question shamelessly.

"I searched your name along with a number of questions. By the end of the night, I had double the number of questions."

His boyish shyness he attempts to cover with a loosely formed fist held over his grin makes me laugh.

"These kinds of questions I think I'd like to answer." There's a hesitation from Zander and I wish he'd stop. "You can ask me anything."

A rawness climbs up my throat, but the pain medicine for

my headache seems to be helping it as well.

"Would you answer questions about your sexuality from Damon as well or only me?"

He had to ruin it, didn't he? There's a hard pang in my chest. Zander has said the quiet part out loud. Staring at my hands, I trace over the lines of my palms and then peer back up at him, offering him complete honesty. "I wouldn't care for questions like that from him."

"But for me?"

My answer is immediate. "I've dreamed of you asking me those questions, Zander." Swallowing thickly, I don't dare to tame my gaze and I don't dare to leave his when I add, "In my dreams, I call you Z."

I anticipate a humorous response, but I'm met with a serious tone.

"You know I watched videos of you. I believe they were consensual but I'd like to hear it from you if that's the case."

"Very much so. My idea, my ... kink. Yes." I remember the first time I shared it. The rush, the desire. "Did you watch them all?"

"Yes," he says and his answer is resolute.

"Then you know that I enjoy many ... tastes." Every nerve ending in my body ignites from the way he looks at me. As if he's sizing up his prey. I'll run from him when he's ready, if that's what he wants.

"Would you care to elaborate?" he questions.

"Elaborate on what? I desire specifics." I am far too comfortable with this man, but it feels nothing but empowering.

"Are you bisexual?" he asks.

"I'm attracted to women, occasionally sexually." I elaborate, because there is a difference between sex and partnership when I think about my attractions. "Romantically, the happily-ever-after type of desire ... I am not sure. I have always wanted men to fill that role. I'm not sure what that says about me, but I'm aware of it. I feel satisfied and ... like I can be complete with a man as my partner. And I do want a partner. A monogamous relationship. But I have always thought women are beautiful, and I enjoy sex with both men and women."

"Understood."

"Do you judge me for it?" I ask, not sure what he thinks of that truth. "In the past, I thought myself to be alone in these feelings. I simply do what I desire and it leads me to want things I don't see people often admitting."

"No. I don't judge you. I understand desire takes many forms ..." His fingers rap along the armrest in a rhythmic beat before he continues his questioning.

"Are you attracted to men sexually too? Or just romantically?" Before I can respond, he adds, "Know that I can help you either way. Your answer will only help me to suit your needs better." His statement is direct. His admission ...

promising things I am desperate for.

Without holding a damn thing back, I tell him, "I'm sexually attracted to you."

"To men," he corrects me, although it's a farce and we both know it.

"Sorry, doctor," I say flippantly, shrugging off my bluntness.

"I told you, I'm not a doctor."

"Sorry, Z," I answer without thinking twice and my treacherous heart hammers at the nickname. *Z.* Peering up, I judge his reaction. "I didn't mean to overstep." His fingers dig into the armrest, and his lips twitch with a smirk. Readjusting on the sofa, the throw slipping down my shoulder and puddling in my lap, I ask, "Would that be all right? To call you Z."

"I would enjoy that very much," he admits to me and there's a crackle between us, one that hasn't spared us during a single interaction.

"If I'd met you at a bar, would you want me?" I dare to ask him. "I've wondered about it since I first saw you. I wondered if you'd fuck me had we met differently."

"I think it may be a matter to discuss at another time, Ella." Zander doesn't move with me in this step of our dance. My body goes so very still as I feel nothing but vulnerability.

"I'd fuck you, Zander. However you'd like. I'd fuck you." I don't allow my gaze to slip as he holds me steady with his, leading me to divulge a truth we've been tiptoeing around. For good measure I add, "Hell, I've already fantasized about it."

"I am obligated to maintain a professional relationship with you." I have no idea how he can speak so coolly, when his gaze blazes like fire and his tone is thick with desire. There is no mistaking that a boundary has already been crossed. A social one. Perhaps a moral one. And neither of us were affected by it. Our boundaries lie elsewhere.

"What a shame—" I start to murmur, readying myself to remove the throw and tell him exactly what it is about him that fuels my interest in him. But I'm silenced and caught off guard as my head whips to the left.

There's only the quick thud of the door that alerts the two of us that someone's here. Just around the corner. Zander's ease is uncanny. His ability to simply slip on a mask that hides every etched detail of the scandalous desire that was on his face just a moment ago is impressive.

With his back pressed against the chair, no one would have any idea of the seduction that nearly prompted me to do illicit and unwarranted things in return for a pleasure I've been dreaming of.

The sudden intrusion would be shocking this late at night if it weren't for the person responsible for it. Kam enters the room like he always does, already talking and as if whatever it is that he has to say is more urgent than whatever's already occurring. He's done it all my life, and in the past I welcomed it. Currently, I'm grateful for his impulsive ways, given the fact that he seems to have failed to notice the energy of the room. "Could we talk?"

My gaze shifts between the two men. "Of course," I answer and swallow, grasping at any sense of normalcy to ground me back in the real world.

"Stay," Zander commands with a subtle hand signal and steals Kam's focus. "Let me leave so you two can have the room," he states, giving Kam a nod.

If Kam noticed the tension between Zander and me, he doesn't let on.

That doesn't change the fact, though, that I feel as if I've been caught. My rapid pulse and wide eyes give it away, if only Kam would look at me rather than watching a very calm Zander leave the room. I catch sight of his hand flexing on the way out; it's the only indication he gives that maybe he's not as collected as he appears.

I have a moment to fix my expression, and I take it. What's happening between Zander and me is mine, mine alone. I need this and I'm unwilling to allow anyone to take it away. It's only once we're alone that Kam takes the seat Zander occupied only moments ago.

He sits on the edge of it, leaning forward and resting his forearms on his thighs. "I had a meeting tonight."

"A meeting." I mutter the words and already feel on edge.

The urgency makes sense. Kam's a buffer between myself and "others." In the past he's negotiated deals, dealt with threats, lawsuits, slander. Anything that would threaten me or my estate in any way.

The times in the past where he's had "meetings" that led to him barging in like this generally meant things needed to change in some form or another. Suddenly all the heat threatens to overwhelm me, and I find myself staring at the fireplace that is no longer lit.

"I've gone over a number of things and I want to start with how to get you back out there," he tells me and that's not at all what I was expecting.

"I wanted to talk about creating routines and maybe ..." He's anxious as he pauses and breathes in deeply, as if what he's about to say is controversial. "Maybe posting again."

There's a small crack in my chest that's raw at the idea of it. It's so very small, though, only a sliver.

"Let's get you together; new hair, maybe?" he offers and I only half smile back at his grin.

"A woman who cuts her hair ..." he begins, and I complete the Coco Chanel quote for him.

"... is about to change her life."

"Just a snapshot, just to tell them you're okay." I nod along with his plan. "What do you want them to know?"

I offer the first words that come to mind: "I'm sorry."

"No, no, no," he says, comforting me. "There is no room

for that. You don't owe them an apology."

"I'm trying."

"I love that about you. I love *you*," he emphasizes. His lips form a thin smile and it's contagious, although the sorrow lingers.

"I love you too."

"I know you do."

"I'm trying," I repeat, then offer as a possibility, "I'm working through it."

"Love this." Kam nods and claps his hands in celebration then adds, "They're going to be so happy to hear from you."

"Can I have my phone back?" When everything happened a year ago, Kam took control of my social media accounts, including changing the passwords.

"... I'll be monitoring comments and moderating as needed."

"You know how it can be. And if anyone comments with the ... video." I shift where I am, feeling this uncomfortable melancholy. Having to live through that moment was the worst day of my life. Having to relive it on social media for months ... well, it almost led to my death.

"If I'm going to talk, I want to talk to my followers. If I write something in that journal, I want them to see it." For the first time in a long time, a burst of motivation urges me to write. "I want to tell them about the ball in the box. It made me feel so much better to know. I want them to know too."

"A ball in a box?" he questions and frustration overwhelms me.

"It's an analogy. More people should know." I've felt the compulsion to post so much in my life, but never so much as I do now. "I can tell them. Even if it only helps a handful of people, I can tell them—" All my life I've shared who I am and what I've gone through on social media. It helped me get through the harder times—most of them—and I know damn well I've helped others get through the same. This is no different. I know there are more people struggling like I am.

"I think right now we should limit what you post—"

"They saw it too. They saw it and other people go through things like that too." My throat goes tight and dry at the visuals that flash in my mind.

"I know they do, love." There's a kindness in his statement, but still a sense of resistance.

"And I want to help them. I want to use my voice and help them get through it. I want to get through it together."

Kam's slow as he takes a seat beside me, making me turn to face him although he's yet to look back at me.

"Kam." I press him, pleading with him. A part of me wants to take back his role, I want him gone and not in charge of a damn thing. I could so easily get the hell out of this house, buy a phone, message someone and they could post on my behalf. He couldn't stop me. He may have changed my passwords, but I'm not locked away anymore.

A chill runs through my blood. Unless I give anyone a reason to send me back. Sickness churns in my gut. "I feel so fucking helpless." The confession is whispered and I look anywhere but at Kam as tears prick my eyes.

"Your love language is acts of service." Kam comforts me, scooting closer to me even though I can't even look him in the eye. "You want to help by doing, but right now, you need to focus on helping yourself."

The sincerity in his message guts me.

"This is a start." Kam's voice is riddled with concern. "Just post to let them know you're trying."

"I want to post about the fucking ball in the box," I practically hiss. I must sound insane; hell, even to my own ears I sound like I'm losing it.

I question why he would silence me. "I've not been on social media for months now. I chose to leave when it was too much. I knew when it was too much for me."

"And then you didn't," he says, and Kam's voice is harsher now. "What if you shared something and you didn't realize what it could do to you … or to someone else?"

"I know there are people who are sad like me. I know that after what happened, I should feel this way. I want them to know I feel it too, and we can get through it together."

"Can we start off slow? Please?" Kam's last word is a whisper, his swallow harsh and paired with a desperate gaze. "I failed you once. I am terrified of failing you again, love.

Please. Please, let's start slow."

"With a single picture and a single sentence … it doesn't feel like it's enough."

"Then why don't we record it. Record what you think is enough and we can keep it, we can hold on to it and post it when you're ready."

"When you think I'm ready," I say to correct him, keeping most of the anger out of my tone.

"Not me, someone better than me," he tells me, his voice pleading. "When a professional thinks you're ready, we can share it."

"Like Damon? If I show him what I want to post?"

"I'm not sure—" he starts and as my jaw drops slightly and my eyes widen, he's quick to take it back. "When Damon *and* myself think you're ready. Damon doesn't know the beast people can be online. You know it. You've been through it."

Pulling one leg up on the sofa, I rest my head on my knee.

"Tell me about the ball in the box," Kam urges me. Tilting my head to the side to lay my cheek on my knee, my silence is met with his plea. "Don't hate me, Ella. I love you. And I am just worried."

I take a shuddering breath in and then let the lone tears fall where they may.

"I think we could post both. Maybe?" he says.

"Both?"

"We could post about the ball, and we could post the

photo. Just … let me do it, all right? I'll post for you. I'll monitor it."

"I really want you to, Kam," I admit to him and my voice is hoarse. "I haven't wanted to, but it feels so important."

"Then we'll tell them. We will. Maybe write it in your journal and other things you want to post. I'll give you a phone, no social on it, but you can take pictures of it, you can text me. You can record whatever you want to share. I just don't want you in the line of fire.

"You know how people can be." Kam's voice is gentle, but his statement is a wrecking ball. I know exactly how people can be.

"This is good," he tells me, his hand on my thigh, giving me a squeeze although anxiousness colors his words.

"What else?" I ask him, brushing under my eyes and counting the last twenty minutes as a win. I will write for them. And he will share it. It's amazing how much relief I feel, yet there just as much exhaustion present.

"We have new hair," Kam says, then holds up a finger after taking a deep breath, "some social media," and another finger is lifted. "What do you think about a shindig?" he asks, tilting his head.

"A shindig?"

He nods. "A shindig." With my smile, he smiles broadly back. "I knew you'd like that one."

CHAPTER 11

ZANDER

Any modifications to a client's plan of care will be carefully considered and vetted by multiple members of The Firm, or outside consultants, or both.

He is her conservator, I remind myself repeatedly as I leave. He has power over her. He has a vested interest. And he could easily take her away from me. Rage simmers although it's merely a product of possessiveness. I'm all too aware of that. So I get up and go.

What the hell else am I going to do? I nod to Kam like the professional that I am—that I will remain—and get up from my chair. "I'll be nearby," I tell Ella on the way out. I don't know why I say it. She knows I'll be close, and so does he.

I can hear their conversation easily from the kitchen. Hiding just out of their view I take a moment to absorb the submission Ella allowed in our conversation.

Kam clears his throat in the sitting room and starts in on social media. *Posting a photo.* He has options for her ... his voice turns to white noise. I don't hear a thing he says. I'm supposed to be keeping an eye on the situation, making a note of what goes on, monitoring her. But I can't. The fact that he's her conservator makes it all the more important.

I need a minute.

I'd fuck you, Zander. I've already fantasized about it.

It's not out of the ordinary for clients to express their fantasies. It's not even the first time this has happened to me. Providing security for a person can heighten their emotions. Protecting a woman ... well, it can lead to harmless crushes. In the past, it has always been unwanted and easily directed elsewhere.

This is different. I cannot get her voice out of my head. Ella was so blunt with those words. So bold. I'm hard as a rock. My entire body is tight with the need for release. To pin her to the wall and fuck her raw.

I've always known this situation was different. From the moment Cade described this contract, I'd known there was a higher chance that the client might develop feelings for one of us, or for all of us. But the way Ella looked at me—

That sure as hell wasn't as "a member of The Firm."

She knows. She must have an inkling of what I'm like, or she wouldn't have looked me in the eye the way she did. Like she knew I could indulge her in a D/s relationship. I could take control and let her breathe. I could give her freedom without worry.

Impossible. It's impossible for her to know those things. There are no videos of me on the internet to give her any suspicion. No videos, but ... I can taste the words on my tongue all over again. The memory of the first command I gave her lingers. *Don't say that to me. Ever.*

I'd ordered her. Commanded her. And Ella's eyes had gone wide for a fraction of a second. Long enough for me to see the desire there. As well as the complete obedience.

I take another deep breath and do what I've been trained to do. I assess the situation. There are no signs of danger. I assess the immediate needs of the client. She seems to want to be speaking to her manager. I assess my position and I find it lacking. I need to get my shit together.

Rubbing my eyes with the palms of my hand, I commit myself to giving her space to absorb our conversation. I will be more direct, more firm in the next.

So I pour myself a cup of coffee. Ella's been preparing a pot before I arrive. It's always hot and fresh when I walk through the door, the scent of coffee wafting from the kitchen.

I know damn well I should announce myself, but I move slowly through the house as I make my way back to them.

Kam's still talking.

"It's just best, babe, if you get back into a routine. Your sponsors miss you, and you know how they are. I convinced them to pause their support instead of dropping you. You have not lost them. Not a single one."

"Thank you, I do know that ... well, I know how they can be," Ella agrees. "You think we'll lose them if I'm ... if I'm not the same?" There's no restraint in her tone, but she's not pushing back at him, either. It sounds like a conversation between two people who know each other very well. Jealousy pushes out against my ribs. Four-count breaths. I only manage one set of four, but it eases the pressure some.

"You might." Kamden's doing his best not to be pushy, but his best isn't good enough. Why does he want her doing sponsorship deals so badly? She's in the care of The Firm. Adding more to her plate right now doesn't strike me as the best idea. But still, I don't interrupt. I do make a mental note to discuss these changes with Damon, or at least ensure Kam's already communicated this with him.

"I'm not sure what all I can do. I don't want to come off—"

"It won't be the same," he interjects, almost too quickly. "Just a few to dip your toes in and remind them you still exist."

Ella does exist.

She called me Z.

My hand tightens on the handle of the coffee mug. I'd kill to hear her say that again. It was familiar and sexy and totally off-limits. She can't use a nickname like that. That's crossing a line.

I know that, and I also know that if she does it again, I won't stop her. I can't think about what I'll do if she announces she'd fuck me again.

"Finances are still steady?" Ella questions. Have I missed part of the conversation?

"Of course, I've taken care of it all. This is ... it's about your security," Kam replies. "It's easier to get sponsorship deals if you already have some. Stay out of the public eye long enough, and you'll be starting from zero. I won't have it. But they're messaging me. They're asking when they'll see a return."

A low laugh. It sends a shock straight through me, from the top of my head to the tips of my toes. Ella's laugh is a broken thing. Her voice is still damaged. But it has a light, sultry ring to it that makes my toes curl again. "You don't think I've been out of the public eye too long already?"

"No, I don't. Really. I think if you jump in now, you'll be just fine."

It's time. I've been standing out here too long, fucking eavesdropping like a child at the top of the stairs refusing to sleep.

I can see her outline as I round the corner. Debating on entering the conversation is ... problematic. It's obvious she's checking to see where I've gone. I watch for it too, the way she watches for me.

It's not good. For either of us. For her, for The Firm.

And ...

We're past that.

I know it in the space of a single heartbeat. I know it down to my bones. I know it from the way my heartbeats turn jagged when I think of her in a room with someone else. When I think of the raw truth in her voice when she said she would fuck me. When I think of her arching her back on that video, with another man's hand around her throat.

One last look into the sitting room. Ella looks slightly better than she did that day in the courtroom, but she needs more than sponsorship deals and talks with Damon and regular check-ins with Cade.

She needs more.

She needs me.

And there's a way to do it.

A boulder shifts off my chest as the idea comes to me. It's like that boulder has been split in two by a flash of lightning. The hairs all over my body pull up tight, goosebumps racing over my skin. There is a way to give her what she needs within the boundaries of the contract. Fuck me. A version of me only weeks ago wouldn't believe what I'm considering.

My cock twitches in my pants. It wouldn't involve sex. It could never involve sex.

The next moment, the boulder comes rocketing back

onto me.

Only this time, the boulder has the shape of fear and guilt and regret. Something insidious and deadly. I turn away from the sitting room and go back to the kitchen. I get the coffee cup down without spilling it, which is better than I expected, and then I brace both hands on the countertop and lean over it.

One.

Two.

Three.

Four.

Four-count breaths.

Four sets of them.

Even. Steady.

Gradually, I control my breathing and my sordid thoughts. Gradually, I straighten. I test my grip by taking a sip of coffee. My hand doesn't tremble with the desire to slap her ass again and again.

That was fucking close.

Too close to the past. Too close by half, and I know what set me off. I know exactly what set me off. It's the decision to offer Ella what she needs. The fact that she wants to fuck me—yeah. That did something to me. It set me up, and now I'm going to have to get myself under control the only way I know how.

I'm still going to do it, but another truth rears its head,

sliding down my throat with the next sip of my coffee.

I'm going to have to talk about this. Not with Ella. Not with Damon, or even Cade, though it's technically my responsibility to consult with them on matters of care ... they don't need to know this. They wouldn't understand, and they could take her away from me. She needs this. I fucking know she does. Instead, I'll consult a neutral third party.

Adrenaline pumps in my veins. There's only one person I trust for advice when it comes to something as important as this. I take out my phone and send a single text message. It's past nine, but the reply comes a minute later.

It's done. The moment I read the text, the duo makes their way out of the sitting room.

I find Kam already stepping into the kitchen, Ella right behind him.

Kam leaves through the back door. "See you tomorrow?"

"Maybe," Ella says. "I'll text you."

"Okay." He smiles for her, big and bright, and then he's gone, leaving a cool autumn wind lingering in the kitchen.

Ella leans against the counter, her huge dark eyes on me. Her hand flits up to her neck. She's touched it less as the time has passed. It's only a brief skim of her fingertips over the hollow of her throat now, the movement almost suggestive. Almost an invitation for me to touch her there. I almost say it. I almost tell her what I've decided to offer her. What I know she needs. I'm almost level with her right now.

"How are you feeling after that?"

The corners of Ella's mouth turn up at my question and my heart slams against my rib cage. Calm focus. I need to have patience for this. I need to talk this out before I say a word to her about it. "Tired," she admits. "Not like last night." She glances off to the side, looking thoughtful, and then her eyes come back to mine. "It's a simple kind of tired. You know?"

"I do." I get that myself with pills. I wouldn't have it at all otherwise. "Are you thinking of heading upstairs?"

"I'm not sure. Should I?"

The charge that goes through me at her words is just as intense as the one that pulsed through me not even an hour ago. Permission. She's already requesting permission. My sweet little submissive. I remind her, if only to give her more space to consider what occurred and to give myself time to ensure I will do right by her, "We had a session. We've talked."

"We were interrupted."

"I know." We were interrupted at the worst possible moment. Or the best possible moment. I don't know which it is. I might not ever know. "There's no rush to continue tonight," I tell her, keeping my voice as level and professional as I can. "If you're tired, we can always have another session tomorrow."

We will have another session tomorrow. I've already decided it. No matter what happens, Ella and I will have another session.

Her lips part, and I hold my breath. If she says it again right now—

"You're right. I'll head up." Her body shifts toward me almost imperceptibly, but then Ella holds up her hand in a little wave. "Good night, Z."

"Good night, Ella."

I wait until I hear her footsteps on the stairs before I sag against the countertop. *Z.*

I wait another five minutes before I take out my phone, dial, and put it to my ear.

"You've got me." It's Silas. He always says "You've got me" when he answers the phone.

"I want you to look into the manager for me. Kamden Richards." Silas has previous experience with military intelligence, and he's the one on our team who conducts the research that can't be done with a simple internet search. "Background check. As far as you can go. Get me a file on him."

There's no hesitation, only a huff of a laugh. "You got a hunch?" he questions.

"I am ... uncertain."

"All right. Need anything else?"

That's the other thing I like about Silas. He's a no-bullshit guy. He does his job, he does it well, and he rarely rocks the boat. "No. Thanks."

We hang up the call, and I bring up the app on my phone that shows me the security cameras. Upstairs, Ella pads from the bathroom to her room and then leaves it. She pauses at the top of the stairs, like she might decide to come back down.

I'd fuck you, Zander. I've already fantasized about it.

After another long moment, she goes into her bedroom and closes the door.

The text comes in while I'm still looking at the camera feed.

Damon: Going through last night's records. Missing a chunk of time off the video. Did you notice any glitches?

I don't answer him.

CHAPTER 12

ZANDER

Any threats to the client will be dealt with quickly and severely.
All legal ramifications will be the burden of The Firm.

The waiting room at 304 Pinewood Circle is the same it's been since the first time I set foot here, in this strip of professional offices. White walls. Black, modern furniture. All of it's comfortable, sturdy, and nonthreatening. No art in frames, just a blue accent wall in the back. I asked Harrison about it at my first session. He said that one of his clients once had a reaction to a watercolor painting, so he stopped displaying art after that.

It takes great effort not to tap my foot against the floor. Moments like this are good for practicing patience. You can't allow the nervous responses to get in the way when you're on a job, and almost no one starts out with enough patience to be that way in high-pressure circumstances.

The soft click brings my attention forward as Harrison opens the door to his office. "Zander. How are you?"

"Good," I answer as I rise, exhaling and preparing myself. "How are you?" I follow him in, nodding at his polite answer. The office is a smaller version of the waiting room, except the furniture is larger and sturdier. I take my seat in a black armchair, and Harrison takes his seat in a gray wingback. Like always, he appears unflustered and calm. Clean-shaven. Dark, closely cropped hair above a neat white shirt and equally neat tie.

"What brings you in today?"

The words I've been planning to say stick in my throat. Harrison is a patient man. He's one of those obnoxiously tolerant people who will outwait you no matter how long it takes. It's one of the things Damon told me about him when he recommended I see him—he knows how to shut his mouth and wait, a quality I appreciate in people more than most other things. "I've had a lot on my mind."

Harrison tilts his head to the side and continues waiting. The clock on the back wall is nearly silent. But there's still a steady ticking sound in the room. Punctuated by my heavy exhales.

No matter how much practice I have at being patient,

he is better. And part of me wants to crack. It's not that I want him to know the details. The urge to keep this secret is strong. It doesn't seem to matter that I decided to talk to Harrison about this—now that it's time, some protective instinct rears up and tries to keep me from saying a damn word. But it's misguided. This conversation is about Ella's welfare. Her well-being is the most important thing.

"We've got a new job. It's different from our typical clients."

"How so?"

"She's a custodial client," I explain. "Released from a mental health facility into our care. For a case like this, the involvement is significant. Around-the-clock presence in her home."

"And this is outside the bounds of what you've done in the past?"

"Well outside. Normally we're dealing with high-profile security and physical threats. For this client—" I almost said her name. I almost said *Ella* to Harrison. It wouldn't have been a disaster for him to hear it. Everything I say in this room is confidential.

But if I say her name to him …

If she becomes part of my sessions as a person in my life and not a client …

That changes things.

I clear my throat. "For this client, the focus is mental health recovery. She was institutionalized for a number of months. This is the stepdown from the Rockford Center."

His left eyebrow raises a fraction of an inch. Harrison isn't the kind of man who's shocked often. Or if he is, he doesn't show it. Could be a trick of the trade, but it could also be his personality. I wouldn't know. I didn't know him before Damon put his foot down and made me schedule an appointment with him years ago. "That type of transfer is unusual, from what I know of the system."

"Highly unusual." There's a strange tightness in my throat, thinking about her standing in that courtroom. "The client herself is unusual, and I think she'll need an unusual approach. If I take that route, I want to make sure I don't cross any boundaries. That I'm seeing the right things."

I'm met with a thoughtful nod.

"And her mental well-being?"

"From what I gather, depressed. Given her medication, suffering with trauma. But very aware, opinionated and independent. She is ... working through her pain, but struggling."

"Is she of sound mind?"

"Yes," I answer without hesitation and feel a heat tingling at the back of my neck. There is no indication from my interactions with her, nor from Damon's notes that she is anything other than a strong woman in the middle of a difficult moment. A moment I could hold her hand through. One of the aspects of her case was the consultant verifying that she was of sound mind enough to leave the center ... but still ...

"What is it you want to see? Something from her?"

"It's not about what I want to see from her." This is harder than I thought it would be. Words are slippery things, and they keep rearranging themselves before I can get them the hell out of my mouth. "It's that I need to look beyond what I want."

"Can you elaborate on that? I don't want to make any assumptions." Harrison doesn't reach for the notepad on the table by his chair. He doesn't so much as look at it. Clasping his hands and resting them on his lap, he waits for me to give him details. He knows better than to write a damn thing down. I don't want any records made of our sessions together. I never have, and I can't allow him to start now.

This is the part I'm going to have to muscle through. Brute force. Rail against. A voice in the back of my head shrieks that this is dangerous, that admitting it is dangerous, that leaning into it is dangerous.

But it's not. Admitting the things I want and need isn't dangerous. What happened with Quincy was a cruel coincidence. It has to have been, otherwise I can't do this with Ella, and I want it.

I more than want it. I need it. And so does she.

"I believe she could benefit from having a stronger hand. Something in line with her previous relationships." He opens his mouth to ask a question, but I speak first. "I'll clarify everything with her beforehand. She's forthcoming."

Harrison steeples his hands in front of him. "What is

it that you're afraid you aren't seeing beyond your own desires for this ... would you call it a Dominant/submissive relationship?"

I don't feel anything like embarrassment when he says it out loud. I feel no shame. What I feel is a certainty that he is the right person to discuss this with, just as I'm certain this kind of mediation would be right for Ella. But that certainty, like all other things, is only a feeling. It's not necessarily the truth. If there's an aspect I haven't considered, then maybe Harrison can help me find it. What I know for sure is that I can't do this—won't do it—without some sort of confirmation. I double-check feelings the same way I double-check the details when I'm working security. Flip every lock twice.

"That's what I would call it, yes. A Dominant/submissive relationship to aid her in a positive recovery." A thousand images flood into my mind of what, exactly, our relationship would look like. There are real boundaries when it comes to D/s relationships. Ironclad ones. And they will have to mesh together with the limits of the contract we're both engaged in. "I've observed her closely. I've talked with her. This approach could help her heal."

"And your reservations?"

"She has past trauma," I say, ushering the truth into the silence. It's an easy quiet here in Harrison's office. He never seems to be in any sort of rush. "I'm sure of that. But she's resistant to discussing it or seek therapy."

"Ah. Much like you were," Harrison points out.

"Yes." I was resistant as hell. I was angry. Grieving. Suffering. Pissed at Damon for making me come here in the first place, and for having the balls to look at the wreck I was and call it like he saw it. I was pissed at him for being right, and I knew he was. When my dad died, I learned the consequences of bottling things up, so damn it, I knew he was right. But that didn't make me less furious. The first few sessions with Harrison were quiet, but not like this. It wasn't peaceful. "It's similar to my situation in that way."

"And you're concerned she could suffer if you aren't—"

"If I don't critically consider every aspect of her care. If I miss something because I'm blinded by my own needs."

My own needs have been screaming at me since the day I saw her in that courtroom, and I would be a fool not to admit that and seek caution.

Harrison considers me, and I know he's taking note of everything. The way I sit in the chair. The expression on my face. The tone of my voice. Even the way I dressed for the meeting. "It sounds like you've already come to a conclusion."

"I haven't."

What I have come to a conclusion about is that Ella would respond well as a submissive. With the right Dominant caring for her, she could heal in a way that aligns with who she is. It's written all over her. But knowing it and choosing to act on it are two different things. I haven't yet made that final decision. Harrison furrows his brow.

I'm adamant when I tell him, "I haven't, Harrison."

"You want me to tell you that you'll be critical in all things and see beyond your wants. You want me to guarantee that for you. You should know better, Zander. There are no guarantees."

"I'm not looking for a guarantee." A match strike of irritation scrapes against the inside of my cheek. I know better than that. I know there are no guarantees in life, not ever, and the worst things that happen to a person seem to appear out of nowhere. It's never the thing you're expecting. Never the thing I'm expecting. "I'm looking for a consultation."

"Then I believe your thoughtfulness reflects a high level of concern for this client."

"Is it your opinion—" I pause to sit up straight and tall in my seat, my fingers tapping on the armrest as I consider my next question carefully. "Is it your opinion that I shouldn't do this?"

The empathy in Harrison's eyes is the one thing about this session that presses at some soft spot I keep hidden. Harrison knows about my past. He knows, because after Quincy, Damon insisted that I seek help. What he actually said was that if I didn't go, he would drag me here himself and sit through the session to make sure I talked. I told him it was against every possible policy to barge in on someone else's private therapy sessions. He'd looked me straight in the eye. "I don't care," he said. "I'll do it anyway. Harrison won't kick me out and I'll kick your ass if you don't."

I believed him. And I ended up here, in this office, telling Harrison things I never thought I'd tell another human being. He helped me sort through the overwhelming guilt and shame.

"It could be what she's missing," I tell Harrison, and I hear it—I hear that note in my voice that I hate. It's the one that's craving affirmation. Just one nod from an outside party to tell me that this is not a terrible idea. That listening to my gut instinct is appropriate for the situation. "It could help her sort through the mess. Give her an outlet that's more inclined to her comfort."

Harrison doesn't laugh. "Because Dominant/submissive relationships are bound by the agreement."

"Yes. There can be a release in it for subs. She—" Shit. I almost did it again. I almost said Ella. I almost spoke her name into this room, and I cannot do that. It's one of the hard limits. She cannot become a part of my life like that. Because of the contract. Because of Cade. Because of me. "She seems to need that assurance."

Ella has been holding herself together in a tight grip for a long, long time. It's obvious from the way she stood in the courtroom and those first days at the house. I know if I took her over my knee, I could unwind part of that tension for her. I've never been more certain of anything in my life.

Fuck.

I am not, *not*, going to think about that in this room. Not when I'm in full view of my fucking therapist.

"I'm not saying you shouldn't do it. What I am saying is that if you're going to move forward, it might be worth calling in backup."

"What do you mean exactly?"

"Having a second person in the room, or at least aware of the situation. Someone else on the team, to ensure there's another party present to measure any differences you might not see because you're so close to this situation."

Someone like Damon.

"I'm keeping a professional distance."

"Of course," says Harrison. "Of course."

"If I were to go through with this ..."

"It would be wise for someone to be aware, in case you are blinded."

"So long as someone else is watching her?" I leave the question half spoken, knowing full well she has a team taking every precaution to monitor her from her sleeping hours to her weekly weigh-in.

"So long as she is in the right mind to consent ... and so long as you maintain your professional distance. You are aware that these relationships can be helpful, but you know they can also bring dependency and other emotions. You must be prepared for that, if that case arises."

CHAPTER 13

ELLA

The Firm will work with the client to arrange for the deployment of partners with best endeavors to conduct the offered services. All personnel is at the client's discretion.

Everything about this moment was intentional. From the way the skirt lays across the sofa, to how I loosely tie the wrap top to show off a little more cleavage. My long-sleeved cotton dress with a floral print in fall tones is new.

Some of the other details may have been for a photo op with Kamden, like actually applying makeup and false lashes. He's just left, snapping a quick picture before leaving through the back door as Zander strode in. But all of it, I chose with him in mind. It's been a long time since I've wanted to dress up and look pretty. Even longer since I thought of a man while doing it.

"You look gorgeous." Zander's statement catches me by surprise. There's nothing guarded about it. My blush rises up my cheekbones and burns at my temples. The things this man does to me is heady.

"Thank you," I whisper, still taken aback as he takes a seat across from me in our blue room of sexual tension. It's what I've dubbed it now that I've spent more time in this room with him playing with fire, than I've been in this room with anyone else since purchasing the home years ago.

"You cut it ... and it's lighter." The manner in which he gives his observation is comical and offers me a warmth I've missed since I told him to sleep well before going to bed last night.

I shrug, as if this all isn't for him, and say, "Blonds have more fun."

"Hmm." His hum is approving, yet questioning all at once. "You're happy with it?" he asks.

"Yes."

"Then I approve," he tells me and I suck in a breath, ready to toy with him. To let him know his approval is irrelevant and I wasn't aiming for it. I'm certain it would get under his skin and he'd flex that hand of his as he did the other night. Before I can usher out a word, Zander takes his normal seat with a seriousness that silences me.

He's wearing his usual black jeans and a matching tee, but there's something different about the air around him tonight. With his thumb moving over each finger, he cracks his knuckles and tells me, "It's been two weeks. I believe there are benchmarks you could meet so long as we establish boundaries ..."

"Boundaries?" I repeat, lifting a challenging brow. I didn't expect him to pick up the conversation right where we left off. Typically he offers me more foreplay than this.

"Yes. And since we're being blunt, I expect you to behave. I expect you to listen to me. Is that clear?" Heat rises through me. Before I can tease him, asking what I'd get out of it, he adds, "I will ensure you are rewarded justly."

"Justly?" I echo the word, feeling suffocated. It's hard to imagine this is happening. That it's real life, this man across from me promising me things only one other man has before. It took ages for James to take me in. Years of occasional fucks, which were enjoyable, but casual, before either of us decided we wanted more. Before we ... got together like this. My throat is dry with the memory but Zander's steady voice commands my attention.

"I need you to agree to that. To listen to me."

"Ever the Dominant, to speak of your needs." I utter the word out loud, so there is nowhere to hide any longer.

"Ever the submissive, to require a strong hand."

Barely breathing, I admit with humor, "I am a people pleaser."

His hum of acknowledgment holds a tone of sarcasm. "Why do I think that only applies to *some* people?"

"That I am selective with who I please?" I ask to clarify, feeling the heat rise to my cheeks. He nods and my bottom lip slips between my teeth as I attempt to recall what my dream was this morning. So I can tell him exactly how I'd like to please him.

"One time my friend told me to have some dignity. She thought sex wasn't a morally neutral act," I comment, reeling in the dangerous tension and focusing on the ends of the throw blanket that have frayed over time.

His eyes narrow and I'm not certain if it's because he disagrees with my statements or not. Either way, I focus on picking barely perceptible lint from the blanket and wait for him to say anything at all. I wait for him to tell me what to do. To establish terms. I wait for him.

"Your rewards will be varied. As will your obligations."

"Is that so?" I push back. I only hesitate for a half second before questioning, putting out the word for both of us to hear it in no uncertain terms, "You can't be my Dom, wouldn't that break the rules? It would breach the contract."

"I have no intention of fucking you while under contract," Zander states firmly, although his cock already straining against his zipper tells me he wants to. "That doesn't mean I can't punish you, that I can't reward you."

"Zander," I say, and I hope he can hear it in my voice. The

temptation, yet at the same time, the caution.

"If you want to give me your submission, I will take care of you. I will help you. I will give you everything you need and more." I'm floored. I've never told a soul. What James and I had … I'd never shared with anyone. Questions batter me, but I obey, gripping the blanket and accepting that Zander knows more than what I've told him. More than what I've told anyone.

It's a sin to fall so deeply into the depths of desire like this. To blindly want, and devour every promise with such greed. And yet here I am. Wanting nothing but this.

"I'm scared," I admit to him and he repositions himself, his fingers intertwining as if he needs to hold on to them to keep from touching me.

"I will never hurt you. We will establish boundaries and limits. I want this as much as I think you do. Tell me if I'm wrong."

Heat dances along every inch of my skin as I confess, "You aren't wrong."

"Then do we understand one another?" he questions.

"Are you sure you can handle me?" I tease him one last time for good measure, wondering what he'll do to me next time I give him lip. Will he turn me over and redden my ass? Will he lean me over the edge of the sofa and fuck me until I beg him to come?

My toes curl and I reach for the throw blanket, needing to hide myself right now although the additional heat is unwanted. Beggars can't be choosers.

"I love your spirit, little bird. But you will only answer yes or no to the following questions, is that clear?" With shortened breath, I answer him yes, because I want to. I am more than willing to consider submitting to him. *Little bird.* I love it. He has no idea what it means to be called *little bird*. A flightless one who used to sing.

As he leans back in the chair, my gaze slips down to his jeans, specifically his cock that presses against his zipper and down his thigh. He doesn't even try to hide it.

"Have you used hand signals before?" he questions.

"Yes."

"Good. This relationship will be between us and only us. Is that understood?"

"Yes."

"I will use signals when we are with company. And you will obey them as swiftly as possible or receive punishment. Is that understood?"

"Yes," I answer and if I ever had any shame, I'd feel it now at my eagerness. Truth be told, I feel nothing but desperation for us to begin. For the first time in a long time, I feel wanted, I feel excited. I feel a heated pulse that's run cold for nearly a year now.

"Show me the commands," he orders. "You have my permission to speak, but only to tell me the commands as you demonstrate them." His deep, steadying breath raises his shoulders and his hands flex on the armrest before he grips them once again. It's heady to watch a man like him resist his own desires. I want to know what will happen when he gives in. When I do what he says and he rewards both of us, fucking me the way he fantasizes about. I'm desperate to know what it'll be like.

Raising my pointer in the air, the other fingers forming a fist, I make a circle parallel to the ceiling. "Undress." I remember the signals easily. The recollection bombards me with the memories of a handsome man who used to care for me like no one else had before.

My pointer over my lips. "Silence."

My pointer directed at the floor. "Come to me now."

My pointer and middle finger both pointed at the ground and touching one another. "Kneel for me."

My pointer and middle finger pointed at the ground but spread apart, forming a *V*. "Spread your legs for me."

With my chest rising and falling easily, I attempt to recall any others, but I don't think there were any.

"And what of specific kneels, eyes down, hands and knees at the point? What of that?"

Shaking my head gently, I maintain eye contact, and question if I should tell him or if I should remain silent.

"You can speak," he states easily and frees me from the dilemma.

"I have never done any of that, and I don't know what 'at

the point' means."

"Was he soft with you?"

Again I hesitate, and my fingers slip to the hem of my dress. "I don't know."

"Did you have lessons from anyone else or observe any other training?"

"No ... not really. It's not ... It wasn't my kink. I love it, and I loved being his, but all I know is what he told me."

Zander's hand flexes once more, the fingers noticeably spreading wide before he makes a fist. My eyes are drawn to the movement. "It means behave."

A smirk tips up my lips. "Is it a threat of a spanking?" I question and Zander doesn't react. Heat overwhelms me, the nervous kind and I stay perfectly still. His hazel eyes never leave me, and it takes a moment for him to answer. "No. It's a command. I will not threaten you, and I don't like that language."

"So serious," I murmur, all humor leaving the room.

"You enjoy being spanked, don't you? You love it even."

"I do."

"When I tell you to behave, it is not the promise of you enjoying what would happen if you do not obey. Understood?"

"Yes."

"Did you have a safe word?" he questions.

I answer with only a nod, the word stuck at the back of my throat.

"Did you use it often?"

"No. I tried not to use it ever." His expression is unmoving, but his eyes spark with an emotion I can't place.

"I want you to pick a word now."

"Should it be the same as before?" I question without asking if I have permission to speak freely. The fear of disapproval grips me instantly and I'm more than aware that Zander notices. It's the first time since we've started that his expression softens.

"We are not in a scene and I am happy to clarify," he answers, his tone soothing and caressing away the worry. "So long as you are answering or searching for an answer, I am pleased." I only nod, my heart continuing to run away from me.

"To answer your question, the word is yours to choose. It can be the same, or it can be different. It can be as simple as 'stop,' although if you choose that word, you may find that you want to change it later ... it's quite easy to use the word when the intensity picks up." With a deeper inhale, Zander's hips move slightly and he palms his erection through his jeans. "I intend to push every boundary with time, but for your word, it is yours and you can use anything you wish."

"Even something like ... daffodil?"

He only nods and when I'm silent in response he asks, "Is that your word?"

"No." My gaze drops to the floral print decorating my

dress. I didn't anticipate feeling … like this.

"What's wrong?"

I nearly shake my head but before I can complete the action, denying that anything is off, Zander commands, "You will tell me what you were thinking. And you will tell me now."

My throat is tight when I answer, "He told me it was a silly word. He said the safe word shouldn't be … daffodil." I don't know why it hurts so much to remember that. James was good to me. And I loved it. I loved everything that we had together.

"He was soft, and from the sounds of it, it was play for you? It was more than likely play for him with … limited experience.

"Safe words are respected regardless of what they are. Whatever word you want to use, I will abide by. Is that clear?"

"Yes." The stirring of heat in his eyes is echoed at my core under the skirt of my dress. Simply from the way he looks at me, with the darker gaze of a Dominant.

"When you are ready, tell me what your word is."

"Pink." I answer him with only the word and not the reason, praying silently that he won't ask for one.

"Pink." He nods once with his eyes closed before opening them, his dark gaze still fixed on me. "Understood."

"You will use this word often because I will be pushing to find your boundaries. I am not a soft Dom. Know that I don't have any indication whatsoever of your limits. Using your safe word is the only way I will discover them. And it will please me when you use it."

That's so different from before. The way we used it ... it was a bad thing to use a safe word. James didn't like it at all, although it only happened a handful of times. I've always thought our relationship was kinky. But now I'm questioning many things I thought I knew well, and we haven't even begun.

"Again, answer me with only a single word. Understood?" The seriousness of his tone is unexpected. For a moment I wonder if this will be too much. If I can handle this, and if this is really what I want.

"Yes."

"For your punishment ... spanking, without a doubt, yes?"

"Yes."

"Orgasm denial?"

I hesitate to answer. With my pause, Zander asks, "You prefer it to be saved for greater offenses?"

"Yes."

"Hmm." The deep hum feels like a threat, like he knows how to mold me, how to make me behave.

"Tell me what your limits are. You can speak freely."

"My previous ..." I trail off and a tickle runs down my neck as I realize I'm going to speak of James as my Dominant for the first time in my life.

"Your Dom," Zander says, then nods in understanding and there's a note of comfort to his tone I don't expect. There's no jealousy. No judgment. It's freeing, although the sadness lingers.

I can only nod and then swallow harshly. "He used forced silence first. Making me request permission before speaking by resting my hand on his thigh."

With a narrowed gaze paired with his thumb dragging across the pads of his fingertips he questions, "For any offense?"

"My typical offense was back talk."

"How is that not surprising?" Zander offers me a wicked grin that teases the sensitive bundle of nerves desperate for his lips and his touch.

"It is important to me that we speak freely and with respect. I love your mouth and there are a number of things I imagine doing to it. But it would hurt me greatly to silence you."

The seriousness of his admission warrants an "understood" from me.

"If it occurs, there will be physical punishment before forced silence. Is that understood?"

"Yes."

"I imagine your behavior was different when you last enjoyed that relationship."

"Very," I admit and the flashes of a woman I used to be threaten to break me. Before the memories can linger, Zander continues.

"There was more than spanking and forced silence. What else?"

My body hums with exhilaration, and I'm grateful for the distraction. "We played with paddles and whips. I loved the paddles. I didn't like the whips at all. I don't want to bleed."

"He broke skin each time with the whips?" Although his tone is calm, his question is spoken quickly, with an urgency that puts me on edge.

"Yes. We only did it the once and I couldn't handle it."

"Not all whippings break skin."

"I don't want to bleed. That's the reason I don't like whips."

The tips of Zander's fingers tap one after the other in rhythm against his jeans as he considers what I've said. "I think we should eliminate all whips for now, but know they don't all result in what you experienced. He practiced and learned with you; is that right?"

I can only nod, emotions getting the better of me. I don't like thinking of James as lesser. There's not an ounce of me that wants that.

"He didn't want to hurt me. He stopped. The moment I used the safe word, he stopped." The words rush out of me, each one of them trembling.

I'm met with silence and the only sound I hear is the blood rushing in my ears.

"I made you feel you had to defend your former Dom. It's not my intention. For that, I apologize."

The unexpected response only brings about emotions I don't expect. A true sadness and I don't want it.

"Tell me what you loved about it with him. Your scenes, the rewards and punishments. I respect and honor what you had with him. What we have will be different. I will be careful in ways I believe he may not have known how to be. Know that I do not think less of him or of what you had because of it.

"I will find your limits. Tell me now if there are any hard limits. Choking, degradation, fisting, bondage, caning, restrictive discipline, cuckolding, anything at all." My jaw drops slightly from how easily he rattles off the terms.

"Cuckolding is me watching while you're with someone else but not being ... tended to myself, correct?"

He nods, his fist resting under his chin now. "Correct."

"I don't want that. I ... The videos may have made it seem like I ..." Frustration bubbles inside of me. "I am not usually so flustered. I prefer to be blunt."

"Take your time," he tells me. "I'm not in any rush."

"I am possessive. I don't want to be jealous. And I'm not, if it's an equal sexual act. But using another woman to punish me ... I am ... I don't care for it at all."

"Cuckolding as a punishment is far different from your kink of exhibitionism and swinging or swapping partners. There's a difference in act, in emotion, in intention. I understand that you can enjoy one and despise the other."

All I can give him is a small nod and a whisper in return.

"Thank you."

"So ... cuckolding is off the table, is there anything else?"

"Bodily fluids in general," I answer.

"Including spitting?" he questions and my body should not at all react as it does.

"No. I meant ... I meant ..."

"Blood, urine and scat."

Pushing my hair out of my face, the frustration turns to infuriation. I am stronger than this. I am capable of answering bluntly and without hesitation.

"I am detail oriented with this information. I understand if you haven't been asked about this before. There is no shame in that."

Again I nod, my lips pressed in a thin line.

"When we enter a scene, I will inform you if there is anything new to us, or anything we haven't already discussed. There will never be any surprise discipline either. Those are the only times I will prepare you. You must use your safe word or even tell me you are considering using it whenever you feel unsafe or an action is unwanted. Understood?"

"Yes."

"And your rewards will be pleasure. Excessive, freely given pleasure. I will test your boundaries, and I will discover what you prefer myself. That is my reward." His voice is firm, and drips with sex appeal. Any negative emotions are quickly burned away by the primitive need that takes control of every piece of me. "You will not dictate your reward, is that understood?"

"Yes," I answer in a whisper.

"Do you have any questions?"

"When will we do scenes?" I ask immediately.

His answer is unexpected. "To start, always." His rough laugh is subdued and a deadly sound. "You're surprised?"

Swallowing thickly, I nod. "Yes." Although I'm slightly shocked, my body blazes with an eagerness to begin.

"You have your safe word, pink. Now I must find those limits in all things. It is best to stay in play for as long as you are willing and I am able."

Adrenaline rushes through my veins and I find myself picking at the tips of my fingers.

"When do we start?"

"When you no longer have questions and acknowledge that you are now mine. My submissive. And I am yours. Your Dominant."

"There's one. I have ... one more question." With his eyes closing slowly, he nods and peers back up at me, still very calm, very soothing in his nature.

"And what is that?"

"Would we record anything?"

He searches my expression, his body stilling. "Like the videos of you I found on the internet?"

"No. Not the ... not the punishments and rewards. That's

not what I was thinking about. Although, I think that's a separate conversation. I mean our sessions. Where we talk. Can we record those?"

"With what intention? You wish to play them back?"

"I want to share them on my social media. Like us talking through it. Not ... not the rewards and punishments. But the therapy sessions. I want to show people how I'm getting through it. The good and the bad. I want to help them too."

"I think we should move through some of the harder topics before we get comfortable with inviting people in. I will consider it, though. I will review first."

A huff of humor that's mostly genuine leaves me. All the men want to review everything. I remind myself that they're protecting me. And I nod although the semblance of a smile slips as I realize something.

"Tell me what's wrong." My focus whips back to him and his stare directed at me holds a possessive intensity that catches me off guard. My answer is immediate and spoken without conscious consent. "My voice."

With a narrowed gaze, I answer more thoroughly before he pries. "It's different than it was before. Scratchier. It sounds different, and they'll notice."

"I see."

There's a small beat in time that passes before he says, "I want you to tell me something about why your voice hurts. Anything at all."

Dread chills any desire I've had over the last hour.

He adds, "I only want one fact but if you want to tell me more, you can. At least one, though. You can do that."

I speak without thinking at his urging, just to get it out there. "I regret it."

"You regret what exactly?" Shifting in this expensive dress on the sofa, I feel cheap and unworthy. "You can change what you want to tell me if you prefer that. But what you tell me must be exact."

"It hurts because I needed surgery after I drank something I wasn't supposed to. I also needed a blood transfusion." I stare at the floor as I speak, focusing on anything other than Zander.

"Look at me," he commands and I do. I obey even though it pains me to do so. "You were aware of what you were drinking?"

I nearly whisper that he told me to tell him only one thing. Just one. Instead the words get caught in my throat, and my eyes prick.

"Good girl," Zander murmurs in a low timbre. Closing my eyes, I do what I've always done, I hold back the tears.

"You have a powerful voice. They will want to hear it even if it sounds different."

I slowly open my eyes to find Zander's expression full of both want and approval.

"If you want to record something, we can. I will be selective about what's saved for you to share."

Pressing my fingers to the corners of my eyes, I comment dryly, "All the men in my life are."

"What do you mean by that?"

"Kam is also monitoring what I post. Damon monitors what I write." For the first time today, my throat feels hoarse and sore; it's definitely gotten better with time. The silence doesn't go unnoticed as I pick up my teacup and drain the now cold tea, leaving behind nothing. It clinks when I set it back down on the table.

It's not until I look back up at Zander that he tells me, "Understood."

Leaning forward in his seat across from me, Zander rests his elbows on his knees and steeples his fingers, resting his chin on the tips of his pointers. "Do you acknowledge that you are my submissive and I am your Dom given the verbal agreements we discussed tonight?"

There is a calmness in his question, but a threat in his hungry gaze.

I murmur, "Yes."

"Say it," he demands.

Swallowing down any hesitation, I give him my submission. "You are my Dominant and I am yours."

He moves all at once, as if my admission opened a lock that held him chained to the chair. So quickly I hardly register it until one hand of his is wrapped around my throat, holding my head against the sofa, with the other on my hip, pinning me to the cushion.

The shock warrants a gasp from me, his touch a smoldering heat.

He stares at my lips as my racing heart pounds in my chest. "What is your safe word?" he questions. "Say it out loud now."

There is no hesitation when I answer him, "Pink." When I swallow, his fingers grip my throat tighter, not constricting, but holding a steady pressure that makes my pulse race with desire.

His right hand moves ever so slowly as he commands me to lift up my dress for him.

My motions are slower than I'd like, but he's patient. The soft fabric glides against my sensitized skin. A low hum that's nearly a growl, of approval resonates from deep in his chest. The air around us is suffocating enough, but his hand on me, controlling me and possessing me, is everything.

I move slowly, but he does not. His right hand cups me through the thin cotton fabric and with his eyes closed he groans, "So fucking wet."

His thumb strums against my clit and I'd throw my head back in pleasure if I could. As it is, I'm pinned where I am.

"You've been a good girl tonight," he tells me, his eyes darkening and holding me still as much as his hand at my throat does.

Pushing the fabric to the side, he runs his fingers along the seam of my pussy lips. Once, twice, spreading the arousal up to my swollen nub where he puts more pressure and runs sweeping circles. Goosebumps race down my arms and then lower.

I struggle to say or do anything, staring at him and for the first time in over a year, feeling wanted. Truly wanted.

When his fingers dip inside of me, not deep, only testing, two things happen at once. My bottom lip drops and I moan from the sudden pleasure. And Zander hisses, "Fuck."

His eyes shut and he stills for a moment. A long enough moment that I question him.

"Do it," I utter and in an instant, he's flipped me over so I'm on all fours. His hand that was at my throat fists the hair at the nape of my neck. His knee is on the sofa, my ass pressed against his jeans. With my back arched, he tugs just slightly.

Again my heart races. He's not gentle with me as he grips my hip, and lowers his lips to the shell of my ear. "Do not test my control, you will regret the punishment immensely."

The battering in my chest is a war drum. "Yes, sir," I answer without hesitation. "I will not do it again."

The desperation for him to reward me, to believe me, not to punish me by denying me this is far too much, far too quickly, is practically palpable. I want him more than I'd ever admit.

A chill meets my backside as he moves away and his grip loosens. For a moment I fear he'll leave me like this, still gasping for breath and wanting. My apprehension vanishes when he pushes his fingers inside of me, curling them and stroking the front wall of my pussy while his thumb brushes against my clit.

My words are unintelligible as I drop my face into the pillow.

His touch is ruthless, and draws out a deep need that's been hidden for far too long.

He finger fucks me until I'm a puddle beneath him, sated and breathless.

I stay as I am, my ass in the air with my dress hiked up and the fabric bunched around my waist after my second release.

The idea of him fucking me consumes my conscience, but he doesn't.

His touch is gentle as he positions me to sit upright. He tells me once again how well I did, then kisses the curve of my neck. My nipples pebble and a shiver runs down my spine.

"Wait here. I have to take care of the cameras for a moment. Then I will hold you and we'll discuss how you'll behave in my absence."

"Hmm?" I question although I have no words and all I can manage is the hmm.

"I'll detail how I want you to fuck yourself and what must happen for you to touch yourself at all when I'm not here.

"We are not done, little bird. We have only just started."

CHAPTER 14

ZANDER

Necessary supervision and adjustments to supervision will be a constant endeavor of The Firm. The client's safety and well-being will always be our top priority.

The autumn night has fallen over the motel, leaving a trail of burgundy and pinks on the horizon. That's my cue to go back to Ella. I had to force myself to sleep during the day. My overactive mind resisted the pull of the pills. It only wanted her. Planning every detail, reviewing potential lines for the next scene. With my muscles coiled, and my imagination going over every possibility, I hardly slept at all.

My body fought again sleep as much as my mind did. My cock wanted Ella, yes, but so did every inch of me. Every last one. Thinking of her sweet lips and her dark eyes lends itself to a strain I'm eager to explore. It pulls everything into a neat, pulsing tension.

Punishing her will have to be enough. Giving her this release will have to be enough, no matter how badly I want to fuck her. No matter how badly I want her to be mine in every way. It'll have to be enough because these are the boundaries we've drawn. Her life. My job. Those are the circumstances, and part of the challenge is finding a way for it to work so that—

My head spins with the recurring memories.

Fuck. I don't want this challenge. I want to have her under my hands and in my bed, and I can't.

Tugging my polo shirt over my head, I grab the file Silas sent over, tucked into a plain manila folder. It's about Kamden, and it's slim. Too slim. I take it with me on the way out to the car and page through it. Kamden has a squeaky-clean reputation. Absolutely nothing has ever been flagged about him in any database anywhere. Silas told me I'd be disappointed if I was looking for something, because there was nothing.

Something's not right with her conservator. It's obvious in the way he guards himself with her, in his language and tone. He's hiding something and I don't like it. I take another set of four measured breaths and put aside my own misgivings about Kam. Even if I liked him, a completely empty file would be suspicious. Ella's got enough of a past to warrant things appearing on a background check. Kam is with her all the time. One of them has a record, and one of them doesn't?

I pull open the driver side door and toss the file onto the passenger side seat, then climb in. The outskirts of town give way to tree-lined streets. Leaves come down and flutter against the windshield like the feathers of little birds.

My little bird is waiting for me in her elegant, modern cage.

If I'm honest with myself, that's what it is—a spacious, comfortable cage. I've never thought about it in quite those terms before, but now I do. I follow the winding road toward the wealthy part of the suburbs where Ella lives tucked away in the mountains, and let myself consider her dilemma. She needs a cage. That much is clear. Only the house is too sprawling. Not intimate enough. The cage she needs is me. The bounds of our agreement.

The irony doesn't escape me. A cage can set a little bird free.

In that space, with her, the rest of The Firm doesn't exist. Nothing exists except the two of us. She can pick up the pieces of her past and study them from a safe distance.

Maybe that's what I'm doing too. Or what I should be doing.

I pull in at Ella's driveway and steer the car around to the parking in the back. Nobody's in the kitchen. One light is on in the sitting room, but she's not there. Not in the rec room, the formal dining room, anywhere.

There's an anxiousness I shouldn't feel. One I aim to remedy when I find her. She's to wait for me in our blue room when she knows I'm arriving. This tense unease that she's not here, not where I left her, not ... okay—that something is wrong—I don't care for it and it's so easily rectified.

"Ella," I call, keeping my voice calm as it travels up the staircase, but is met with silence. Where the hell is Damon? Distress spurs my steps to pick up.

I climb the stairs. The door to her bedroom is open, but it's empty.

Where are they?

Did she tell them? Was it too much and she's backing away from me? It's a bitter reality to imagine. Of all the things that kept me up, this wasn't one of them.

Checking my phone, there are no messages from Damon and I'm nearly five minutes early. Still, where the hell are they?

There's only one place I haven't been in this massive house. One place that Kam fiercely guarded when we were doing the modifications. Swore up and down that he'd keep it under control, but we weren't allowed to move anything, to replace anything. So we didn't. Instead there's a rope that's anchored in the doorway of the west hall.

It could've been a mistake, listening to him. That empty file makes me uneasy all over again. I move through the halls to the west wing, ducking under the thin rope and ignoring it altogether.

It's an eerie feeling that surrounds me when I flick on the light. I don't get more than a few steps in before it dawns on me that if Ella were here, she would not be okay.

The clearest demarcation is the art on the walls.

Every piece is wrapped in paper and a thin layer of packing foam as if it's been protected in order to move it, but nothing has been moved. It's all still hanging in place with a thin layer of dust coating it. Like an abandoned house, still filled with its memories and bundled up safely but kept hidden.

The hairs on the back of my neck stand up.

I must have seen this before. I must have. I remember the conversation with Kam, his body blocking the entrance to this hall. I must have looked past him and noted the artwork, but I don't remember it. That was the day of the court hearing, shortly after and before the informal introduction to her downstairs.

I had still been rattled from seeing her.

That's why I didn't notice the artwork. It would have already been done by then.

There's too much packing tape for me to unwrap one and see what needs to be protected like this. Protected—or hidden.

Even the silence is different in this part of the house. As if it hasn't been disturbed in some time, and doesn't like to be disturbed. Not that houses have feelings. I'm not superstitious enough to believe in shit like that. All I know is that the quiet presses in harder the farther I go. Three more steps.

"Ella?"

I call her name, but I already know she's not back here.

The first door creaks as it opens. I know she's not here. I can sense it. All the time I've spent working in security has fine-tuned my attention to spaces. They breathe more when someone is there. Small movements in the air give them away. There is no movement here, only a deep hush.

That's when I hear a creak behind me.

The new current in the air reaches me a second before Damon's hand does. A strong hand, just above my elbow. I have just enough warning to tamp down the instinct to subdue him. "We're not supposed to be back here."

I turn to face him, shutting the door as I do, and Damon's expression is more serious than I've ever seen it. Worry flashes in his dark eyes, and a crease in his brow confirms the feeling. I know we're not supposed to be here. He knows I know. So I don't bother saying a damn thing about it.

"What do you know about this wing of the house?"

He releases me and takes a half step back, staying close enough that we can keep our voices low. "Damn it, Zander, why didn't you read the file?"

"Because I never read the files." Irritation is evident in my answer, but it's short-lived. I could have searched other areas of the house before I came in here. "And she asked me not to."

He holds my gaze and I see it—I see it. *Suspicion.* A shiver grips me. Does he know about the arrangement I have with Ella? Has he already figured it out? Damon, of all people, would be the one to notice. He's here at every shift change, since we're paired for this job. He sees me the most. And he knows me the best.

I could tell him, here in this too-quiet hallway with the strange wrappings on all the artwork. That was the suggestion Harrison made, and he had a point. Telling Damon would protect The Firm.

But I keep my mouth shut.

I'll sort through the why of it later, when I'm alone. I'll come up with a plan. But I'm not going to tell him now. Not when I crave her so much that my chest hurts. Not when my hands ache to touch her again.

Not now.

"This is the main wing," he says finally. "Where she sleeps now is the guest wing."

It explains the hotel-like quality of her bedroom. I've noticed the richer the client, the less clutter in general. They can afford a cleaning staff to keep it neat, and the items they buy tend to be fewer but better quality. Still, they have small details that belong to them as people. Who they are and what they cherish most. Ella's room is devoid of almost all the personal items I'd expect. I should have known it wasn't just because of her wealth, or her status. I should have known there was a deeper reason.

She sleeps in a room that's not her own, while her memories are locked away behind packing paper and dust.

"Because all this is too much for her."

"Yes," Damon agrees, although then he adds, "Potentially. The circumstances might have changed. Her progress has been consistent. Ella's taking her meds and having longer conversations. She's more active during the daytime than she was before she was admitted. We spent some time in the yard today, talking as we walked."

"Yard" is an understatement. The estate is grand with a sprawling lawn in the back, fenced in white and bursting with plants and gardens and a chestnut tree. It must sit on at least two acres and backs up to a picturesque mountainscape. I haven't been out there with her much as the fall is rather bitter and she seems to prefer our blue room.

"How did she handle that?" It's hard to picture her out in the sun, strolling with the dappled light in her hair. Her face tipped up to look at the clouds. Her fingertips brushing over a hedge going brittle with autumn. What I really want to know is if the sun warmed her up. If she seemed free on the outside, or if she was still a little bird in a cage.

Damon can't tell me that.

He nods, considering. "She did well. We took it slow."

He's protective of her too ... and for the second time in the space of this few minutes I think about confiding in him. Because the Ella he describes, this woman who needs to move slowly in the yard, this delicate, fragile thing—it's not the Ella who looked me in the eye and consented to spanking with a gleam in the dark centers of her gaze. There are many sides to a person's humanity. Damon is willing to help her, and he can help her in ways that I can't. If I can offer insight, I should. If it will help her. Only if it would help her.

She's stronger than she appears. But also … maybe more broken than I'm seeing.

"And the conversation? Did she share anything I should be aware of?"

"No," he says and shakes his head. "Just small talk mostly. But she's opening up."

"That's good." I force myself to focus and get out of my thoughts. "Where is she now? I was looking for her."

"Resting in one of the guest rooms." I walked right past those doors on the way here. Didn't even bother to look because I thought she'd be in her own room. "She came up about an hour ago. I think the curtains are thicker in one of the other rooms." He shrugs.

I follow him, talking as we go.

"She's been more tired recently," he says.

"She's been staying up later, maybe till two or three."

"Really?" Damon seems surprised. Our footsteps are heavy as we descend the staircase.

"Yeah." I don't elaborate although his gaze is prying. "What time is she waking up?" I question.

"Around nine. I guess that's why she wanted a nap."

"What time did she lie down?"

"'Bout … two hours ago maybe?"

We go downstairs to the kitchen and Damon shrugs on his coat. I try to ignore the disappointment gnawing at my gut. I wanted to see her. I wanted to hear her voice. I want to know what she sounds like when she whimpers because her ass is red and she's falling into that loss of control.

With his keys jingling in his hand, I decide to wait for him to leave and then I'll prepare to wake Ella. We have more boundaries to set. "Wanted to talk to you about something," Damon starts as he pats his pockets, checking for his keys and his wallet. Tension pulls my spine tight. *Damn it.* This is the moment he's going to tell me he knows about Ella. That he saw the way I looked at her in the courtroom. That she spilled to him the details of our arrangement. I brace for it. I'm not ashamed. It's what she needs.

"Go ahead." I hear myself say it, and I'm proud of how normal I sound.

Damon leans against the kitchen island. "I heard you paid Harrison a visit."

Well, shit. I should feel relief, but it's only slight. "Yeah? Did he tell you that?"

"He mentioned that you stopped by. You know he doesn't give details—he only mentioned it in passing. He said he was glad to see you."

"Okay." What is this conversation? "Is there a question in there?"

"Are you okay, man?" Damon's tone is genuine.

Empathetic. It's what makes him a favorite of our clients. "We haven't spoken about the hearing yet, and I know it has to be eating at you."

The air sweeps out of my lungs. Of course. The hearing. My gaze drops to the floor as I get ahold of my bearings and then look him in the eye to answer, "I'm doing all right. It'll be better when it's all over."

"I know it won't bring her back, but—" He shakes his head, looking off toward the kitchen window. "She deserves resolution. As much justice as she can get. So do you."

My throat goes dry and I busy myself making a pot of coffee. That familiar ache returns. I'm comfortable telling Damon the truth. That's why it slips out of me now. I'm not used to holding back with him. He's seen me at my worst. "You think she'd want me to have closure? Sometimes I think she wouldn't want that, since the whole damn thing was—"

"Don't say it." Damon holds up a hand. "It wasn't your fault."

He allows us to sit in silence for a moment, the only sound being the drip of the coffee maker. I take a deep breath, then another. Four-count. And then do it again.

Finally I respond, "I know." Don't I fucking know. I've worked through this with Harrison. I'm done working through it. And then a moment like this comes along and all those doubts are back in my head. I remind myself what happened is a ball in a box. "I know. But it feels like the blame should be mine."

"No, man. Quincy wouldn't want that. It didn't matter how things were between the two of you. What happened wasn't your fault. If it was, you'd be the one on trial."

Quincy was good. She was a good person, and I didn't trust her to know what she wanted from me. I didn't trust myself to be honest with her about what I wanted. It's what drove us apart in the end. That and the fact that we just weren't right for each other.

"Look, I'm here." Damon slips his hands in his pockets. "I need to get out of this house and find some food, but—" I laugh at him in spite of myself. "I'm here. You know?"

"Yeah." I clap him on the shoulder. "Get out of here."

He goes, leaving me in the silent house and waiting on Ella so I could feel something other than the emptiness I feel right now.

CHAPTER 15

ELLA

Team members of The Firm will work closely together to provide a consistent and reliable care experience.

"If you brought donuts, I'm going to guess it went well?" The early morning light is still painted with a mauve hue as the sliding back door closes. Kam wears his million-dollar smile, as I used to call it, just as well as his custom-tailored gray blazer with designer jeans. "By the way, you look hot," I add and bring the mug of tea to my lips.

"I would say it went exceptionally well." With his statement, Kamden offers me the pink box of sweets.

Setting down the cup, my smile grows. "Tell me they had the double glazed?"

He speaks as I lift the top, eyeing a half dozen chocolate donuts and inhaling the fresh, sugary scent. It's heaven.

"You know it, my love," he says, then hums and drags out the chair to the left of me, scooting it closer and taking a seat. The extension off of the kitchen boasts large windows. Damon suggested I have my morning tea here to soak up more sun since the weather has turned bitterly cold this week.

Slipping off his sunglasses and folding them, Kamden comments, "I'm surprised you're up this early."

"Couldn't sleep," I answer without thinking. It's the truth that sleep evaded me, but it's because Zander left my mind reeling last night. My nap went longer than I'd have liked and by the time I woke up, he had a list of tasks for me. Starting with me writing down every desire I had for him and reading them off to him one by one after leaving my panties elsewhere. He had me lay the throw blanket across my knees, and then spread my legs. It offered him a view to say the least, but all the cameras would see is me reading from my diary and Zander sitting calmly, asking questions for me to detail more of my goals, desires and fantasies.

He didn't touch me once. Not a single time last night. Instead, after hours, he left me with the task to think beyond what I'd written and focus on what would please him most. Once I write that down, he said I could pick whichever fantasy I wanted.

What would please him most? If I confided in him about

what happened. I'm almost certain that's what he wants from me.

The disappointment still lingers I pluck a chunk of the sugary chocolate sweet and pop it into my mouth.

Kam's tone is serious when he asks, "Do you want to talk about it? I can get you stronger sleeping pills, or get the doctor over here to discuss the current medication." As he leans forward without a trace of his humor, the bags under his blue eyes are clear as the morning sun.

"No," I answer with just as much surprise as kindness. "No, no." I wipe my hand on a cloth napkin and shake my head. "It's umm, the medication is working well I think and that's what Damon tells me. It was just a long night really."

My attempt to ease his worries doesn't appear to sink in.

"You'll tell me if you do need anything, right?" he questions and his gaze slips to the old brick of a phone that's capable of making calls, but doesn't have any function for apps. I text him and only him really on it, although I have a small handful of friends I trust whose contact information is on it as well.

"Of course I would. You know if I want to annoy anyone with my bullshit, it will be you," I joke.

He snorts, seeming to relax and leans back in the chair. "It's not annoying and it's not bullshit, but yes," he says and smirks, "I do know how you love to torture me."

I mirror his relaxed posture and ignore my exhaustion as I say, "So, the posts went well."

With his left hand tapping his sunglasses on the table, Kam nods. "Both went well." He emphasizes the first word and it doesn't make much sense at all that I should feel emotional about it. About the knowledge that he did post about the "ball in a box" analogy.

"Was it helpful?" I question, the mug in my hand halting midway as I wait for his answer.

His nod is enthusiastic. "So many people could relate," he tells me and then adds, "There are some comments with other suggestions as well, but I wanted to run them by Damon before showing you." His smile dims slightly, but he holds it in place. "Just to make sure I'm not telling you something or spreading something that could be—"

I cut off his explanation with a wave of my hand through the air. "I get it. You want to make sure it's helpful before I go believing someone off the internet."

His smile turns tight and his gaze drops.

"I should call you Daddy Kam."

"Oh," he says as his brow raises and his voice is playful, "don't tease me." His joke is followed with, "Besides, according to your other post, you've already got a Daddy."

He holds his phone out for me to see.

It takes me a moment to register what I'm seeing. The photo is one that I remember telling Kam I loved. The sight of the floral dress brings back the memories of it being flipped over my waist while Zander finger fucked me. The rumble of his words, *do not test my control,* nearly has me shivering in my seat.

Focusing on the rest of the photo is much easier.

My caption reads: *I am trying. I am working through it. And I am sending love to all who are working through whatever has stolen their smile.*

I love it. That is exactly the message I would send had I done it myself. Taking a sip of my tea, I notice there are only three comments on the screenshot of the post, which has over a hundred thousand likes on it in the ten minutes that had passed since he took the screenshot.

The first: Sending you so much love back!

The second: I am so proud of you. You can do this, you sexy thing, you!

The third: Whoa, check out the Daddy in the background. I'll work through anything to get to his fine ass.

My eyes widen as I read it and I have to take a look at the photo again. My heart pounds and my blood heats.

Kamden doesn't hold back his laughter at my reaction to the sight of Zander in the background of the photo. The black shirt and jeans he was wearing that day aren't doing him any justice as he stands in the corner of the background through the windowpane. His focus is ahead as he prepares to enter through the back door, so it's a profile.

His stubbled jawline and the power that radiates off of him, even from just striding across the back patio, is sexy as fuck.

"I mean ... they're not wrong."

A heat travels across the back of my neck. I'm not certain I can remain composed, so I down the cup of tea before I speak.

"They aren't wrong," I say, my tone less flippant this time.

"You going to start calling him 'Daddy' now? The term going around is 'lover boy,' just so you know."

"Lover boy?" I can hardly get the words out considering the way my breath has been stolen. He's my secret, my safe place. "I didn't realize he was in the picture."

"I think it was one of the last ones I took," Kamden tells me, laying the phone on the table. "It's been great for image. Everyone loves a scandal and even more than that, a romance."

"What did you tell them?" My inquiry comes out more breathy than I'd like, but there isn't an ounce of suspicion from Kam.

"The official statement from your estate is, 'We are incredibly grateful for the professional guidance The Firm has offered during this time of healing.'"

"Professional." I nod in agreement of his wording.

"If you remember, I've always been the professional one. It would be you who would have commented something like, 'Yeah, but is he packing,' along with the eggplant emoji."

The laugh that bubbles up is genuine and given Kam's reaction, the hints of worry diminish quickly enough.

"Now that's a beautiful sound." Damon's comment comes

from behind us and I turn to see him making his way over from the other side of the island. His kindness is never unnoticed. The man knows how to make me smile too. I appreciate it and I make sure to widen my grin when I meet his gaze.

"Just the man I wanted to see," Kam pipes up. As the two of them have a quiet conversation, I assume about the comments Kam wants to show me referring to the second post and hopefully not the first, I busy myself with making another cup of tea.

My journal is next to the kettle. Flipping through the pages I find the last one, which I titled: *What would please him most?* It's no coincidence I chose to use a hot pink gel pen for this page. The rest of it is blank.

Damon saw me staring at it this morning. I peek up at him as I wait for the kettle to whistle, and he and Kam are focused on Kam's phone. Occasionally Damon nods.

He told me I was doing well. He said I should be careful not to rush things or judge my progress harshly.

A bad moment is not a bad day. Not being able to complete a task doesn't mean failure.

Staring at this blank page, though, I'm not sure Zander will agree.

CHAPTER 16

ZANDER

Each client of The Firm will receive regular evaluations to determine whether progress has been made toward their individualized care goals.

Ella's hair is wet from the shower when I arrive for the night. I catch the scent of her shampoo the second I walk in the door, and it's all I can do to listen to Damon as he recaps the day. He said it was a lighthearted day but those days worry him. After the highs come the dips, and oftentimes they can feel like falling back when they're only natural.

Harrison once described it to me as a spiral staircase built against a wall. Even though we climb higher and higher, we still hit the wall. We must. It has to occur to move onward.

Making a mental note, I debate on whether or not I should carry through with my plan for tonight.

"Should I aim for an uneventful, quiet night then?"

Damon's head shakes. "Take her lead. If she wants another long conversation, I wouldn't avoid that. It may be necessary. You good?" he asks.

Nodding in agreement that it may be necessary, I continue the movement with my answer, "I'm good."

I send him on his way and find Ella at the archway to the kitchen. I'm not sure where she was before, but she's here now. "Hi," she says softly. The cadence of her voice and the shyness in her posture already have me rock fucking hard.

There is something about a strong-willed woman's submission that is utterly addictive.

"My little bird," I murmur and each word is practically a hum from deep in my chest. I purposefully make the satisfaction audible and I'm rewarded with a slight blush that rises from her chest up to her cheeks.

"We'll start tonight with a scene."

Ella stares at me, her large dark eyes sparking with desire. She nods, and I know she feels what I feel right now. Pent-up need. It's been a long twelve hours without her.

And I am desperate. Combine that with exposed skin revealed by the pale pink silk robe she dons that hugs the small of her waist and cuts off mid-thigh ... fuck me.

Now that I've had my fingers in her sweet, tight cunt, it's

practically all I can think about. I can and will keep more than one thing in mind at once. Like her safety. Like her progress. Like the way her body moves as we go to the sitting room. But damn does the thought of her enjoying my touch like she did, getting her off and rewarding her occupy every quiet moment.

She takes her seat across from me, perched and waiting for demands like the eager sub she is, and I adjust the lighting in the room. One lamp, turned down as low as it will go. The flames in the grate licking at the crystals in the fireplace. It's intimate, the way I like.

I take my seat. "Stand."

Ella does so without hesitation, getting to her feet in a graceful motion that I want to follow with my hands. The desperation I felt walking in is already waning. It's a combination of the low lighting and the fact that when she obeys me for the first time, we are in the scene, I am in control, and this is right.

It feels right. A 24/7 power exchange is already difficult when there are large gaps of time between scenes. Add in the other men and their own power over her for necessary reasons ... every time I walk away there's a prick of nervousness that they won't care for her like they should and that our efforts will be lost. So as much as I'd like, this arrangement is not perfect.

"What are you wearing under your robe?"

"Only panties."

"Take them off." My command, evenly and calmly spoken, is given with my palm up.

Again she obeys, approaching my seat with careful steps and placing them into my outstretched hand. When this is over, she can have them back. Her dark eyes are luminous in the firelight, and she's so close that I can scent her. Fuck, she smells good. Everything about her is intoxicating. It's a combination of her light, floral shampoo and her skin beneath that.

"You can sit down now."

Only a mild hesitation—a fraction of a second before she turns and walks back to her seat. My cock strains against the front of my pants. I ignore it. It's more difficult to dismiss when I'm not with her.

"Good girl." My approval brings back the simper she wore moments ago. "There are things we need to discuss tonight. For this, I'll allow you to speak freely. Understood?"

Ella nods, and I imagine it's because she's conserving her voice, the way she always does. "How is your throat today?"

"Better," she answers confidently.

"Good."

She folds her hands demurely in her lap, resting them on the silk fabric of her robe. Her knees are kept firmly pressed together. I could make her spread them, but I don't.

"You have events scheduled. A brunch, and a rendezvous

with executives." I pause, gauging her unmoving expression. Kamden's details are scant. All he noted was that they were friends of hers she hasn't seen in far too long. Damon agrees that she should be socializing. A "rendezvous" isn't a good enough description as far as I'm concerned, but I've been tasked to handle both of them, at Kamden's request.

"Are you looking forward to them?"

"I am." Ella's gaze softens and she seems to doubt herself a moment but then finds her voice I know to be strong. "It's been too long and I miss my friends." The relief that spreads through my chest is unexpected. I hadn't realized how much I dreaded pushing back on Kamden's request, and Damon's approval, if Ella had been anything other than happy to attend. The idea of her with friends, laughing, smiling and joking ... I want that for her.

"It will be a delight to see you among your peers."

"You'll be going?" Ella's surprise forces a smirk to my lips.

"That is correct. You seem shocked."

"I just ... I was under the impression Damon would be with me during the brunch, since it will be during his shift. Did you request it?" There's a mix of both hope and worry in the vulnerability that lingers in her question.

Shaking my head once, I admit, "I did not. Kamden did."

"I see."

"Would you rather I didn't?" I question, not understanding her concern and not liking it either.

"It's a relief you'll be there, to be honest. I just ... Kamden didn't tell me that."

My hum of acknowledgment is low and short.

"There will be alcohol present at both. It's my preference that you don't drink at either event. Do you agree?"

Ella meets my eyes. Her lips part, as if she's considering disagreeing deeply, but it's several beats before she speaks. This consideration tells me that she's capable of being in this scene. It's something I check for constantly—her ability to consent. Consent, in scenes and otherwise, is never one and done. It can change at any second. At any moment, she could give me her safe word, and this would end. "Yes. I agree." Her voice is so low, so soft.

"I know about the small bottles, little bird."

A frisson of shock moves through the air between us, Ella's eyes widening.

"Do you know which ones I'm referring to?" I ask.

She only nods. "I'd like you to answer verbally."

"I do. Yes."

"I found the bottles, and I reviewed the tapes. I know what you did, and I don't like it. Self-medicating and risking adverse side effects is something that puts you in danger. You're not going to be drinking while you're in my care. I'm glad you agree to the rule. But you should know that I will punish you if you break it." My grip tightens on the armrest when I add, "Severely, and you will not enjoy it."

She nods again. Ella rubs her knees against one another nervously. Her body is tight, not with desire, but fear. "Am I in trouble?" She hasn't experienced a punishment yet beyond orgasm denial. I set her up for that one last night. Tonight I intend to set her up again, but it will be different and certainly not for something she did before she gave her submission to me.

"Do you think you should be?"

"I was ... it was a bad moment."

"We also hadn't established our arrangement yet. Had we?" I question her.

Shaking her head, her posture relaxes just slightly. "No, we hadn't started."

Taking a moment to let her compose herself, I shift in my seat, not hiding how very hard I still am for her. I need her to know I still want her. Even if she's done something to upset me, I will always want her.

"Now. We need to prepare for your outings. We will practice."

"Practice?"

"Questions will naturally come up while you're with your friends, or while you're at the rendezvous." Ella changes before my eyes. Her breathing goes shallow, her back straightens and her muscles tense. "They may ask you questions about your voice, or other specifics you have yet to discuss openly and you'll need to be prepared to answer. We'll practice that now."

"They won't ask. They won't." Ella denies the possibility

and it fucking guts me how much she truly believes it.

I continue with the scene, I continue my role as her Dom even as the emotions sweep through me. "If they ask you why you hurt yourself, what will you answer?"

"No." Her answer is hard. She struggles to keep my gaze, her head held high in defiance. "I don't want to do this."

What she hasn't done, though, is use her safe word.

"You know what to do if you want to stop something. If you want a scene to end without punishment. You know exactly what to do. So are you telling me no?" I gentle my voice to add, "Or are you saying something else?" She has yet to use her safe word. I imagine the first time will be the hardest for her. This moment, though, this scene, will hopefully not be what does her in, but given her state, I need to remind her that it is available. She has yet to discuss it with me, and it could very well be a boundary and a hard limit for her.

She holds my gaze, the cords in her throat tightening as she whispers, "No."

Good girl.

It does something to me, that "no." That open disobedience. I don't let it show on my face, or in my posture. Her choice tells me how much she wants to heal. That is my good fucking girl. Even if she's going to be punished, I am thrilled with her decision.

"No?"

"I don't—I don't want to talk about it."

The energy in the room feels heightened, almost electric. We're heading toward a line, together. We're barreling toward something new, and I can't breathe for the anticipation of it. I study her. The way she sits, her back straight, her chin lifted. The way her dark eyes never leave mine. Ella knows what she's doing.

"You need to practice. It can't be avoided." It's true. When she reenters public life, the question will come up. More than likely, given her public profile, she will endure it constantly. She must prepare. I need to know she can handle it. I need to know that it won't cause her to break down and erase all the progress she's made. "Are you choosing to disobey me?"

Her chin lifts another fraction of an inch, and then she nods. Definitive. Yes.

"And you're aware of the consequences for disobeying me."

Ella clears her throat. "I'd rather be punished."

I could burst into flames and take this chair with me, and the house, for how much I want her. If I weren't bound by a contract, I'd blister her ass with my palm and then fuck her over the edge of the sofa. Instead, I don't make a move. If she's going to do this, then it will remain her choice all the way to the end. "I won't allow you to deny me indefinitely, little bird. Do you understand?"

"Yes."

I shift forward in the chair to give myself the room we'll need. "Then come put yourself over my lap." Her breathing quickens, audibly so in the quiet of the room, but Ella gets to her feet right away. There's the slightest shake to her body as she crosses the room. She's nervous. Which only makes me harder. My cock twitches with need, begging to satisfy her. Ella hesitates at my knees, and I put a hand on her hip. A professional touch. "Bend."

She does, arranging herself over my lap. I help her into the position I want for a spanking before bracing my forearm over her lower back. She's so warm and soft over my thighs. So nervous. So brave. I slip my hand over the back of her thigh, just above her knee, letting my fingers trail there. The goosebumps aren't my only reward; she shivers and writhes ever so slightly. "You know you can end this," I murmur into her ear.

Ella shakes her head. "No." She swallows. "I want this," she whispers.

I know she does. She's wanted it for a long time now. Her body is begging for this. To have some sort of closure for a pain she can't control. "I know, little bird." I slide my hand up the back of her thigh and under the hem of her robe, and then I flip it up, exposing her ass to the air. She shivers again, and I know it's not from cold—the fire has made it more than comfortable in here. I test one cheek with a quick slap, then the other, rubbing slow circles over the flesh. Her ass is gorgeous with my marks on it. So easily coloring for me. It'll be red by the time I'm done and she'll remember this every time she takes a seat, or even so much as shifts in her seat tomorrow.

Clenching my jaw, I prepare myself. It's been far too long. "Toes on the carpet," I direct her. With the adjustment, her ass lifts into my hand. "You'll keep them there until I'm finished. You can make noise if you need to, but you won't get up, and you won't kick your feet. Understood?"

"Yes."

A breath goes out of her. This is familiar territory. My little bird knows how to do this. I trace my fingertips along her slit.

"Thighs farther apart."

Ella obeys, and it's my turn to take a four-count breath. Her submission brings out a carnal need from me, and it's also more than seductive. She tempts me like no one ever has, and yet I have to be so fucking careful with her.

I position my palm over her ass so she can feel it. "Thirty swats," I tell her.

"Thirty?" Her whisper betrays her lack of confidence.

Without her able to see me, I don't hide my smirk. "I told you I wasn't a soft Dom. I won't make you count out loud this time, but you should do so in your head."

I give her a beat to process it, and then I begin, sucking in a breath as I slap my hand down on her heated flesh without holding back. She whimpers through clenched teeth for the first three. The next five, though, her mouth drops open and the whimpers are louder, but still short. On the tenth one, her ass is lovely shade of red. It's a dizzying color. The color I've seen in my dreams and my fantasies.

Squeezing her left cheek, I check on her. Wide eyed, she stares at the floor. Her expression isn't scrunched; there are no tears. "Look at me," I command her and she does so. Immediately. Her face is flushed, her chest rising and falling with exhilaration.

"Do you know how many are left?" I question to gauge her ability to consent. Shock can steal a submissive's voice. When she answers twenty, I'm more than aware that she's still with me.

At fifteen she lets out a little yelp, and my cock twitches beneath her. It sounds exactly like I imagined it.

At twenty, her head lifts, and she strains against my thighs, pushing back on my forearm that holds her steady. But she doesn't try to stand, and her toes stay on the carpet. Fuck, it's sexy. I can tell how badly she wants to kick. She's close to crying but not as close as I thought she'd be.

She groans under me and when I ask her again how many, this time her brow pinches, and she can't control her pitch as she calls out ten.

"Good girl," I tell her and reward her by letting my touch fall to her slit. It's a short moment of reprieve. My little bird can take more than this.

But I won't push her tonight. She's already had her first

punishment; I would prefer it not to be paired with the first utterance of her safe word as well.

I finish the final ten spanks with the same even rhythm, not letting up, not going soft, but also spreading the blows so they don't land on the same spot too many times in a row. They're hard cracks of my hand on pink flesh, but I'm certain they won't bruise her. Ella cries out with each one but no tears slip from her eyes.

Next time I will be more severe with her. And knowing Ella, next time will come sooner rather than later.

I deliver the final blow and she shudders over my lap, gasping. I pull her upright over my legs so she's straddling me. It's so close to how she'd be if I could fuck her like this. If she was mine. With her robe loosened, her left breast is exposed and I indulge, quickly dropping my lips to her nipple. It's a quick suck that I release with a pop, and then I take her chin in my hand and guide her face up so she's looking into my eyes. "Will you disobey me again?" I ask her even though I'm well aware she will.

My own breathing is heavy, but hers is much worse, it's ragged.

She gives me an adamant shake of her head, and I could kiss her and that naïve, eager-to-please mouth of hers. Her eyes drop down to my shirt.

Squeezing her ass in my hands, I let her small body drop forward as she moans, bracing herself on my shoulder.

"Look at me." Every time she does this—every time she brings her dark eyes to mine—I feel it. An electric jolt. It's deep, in my veins. Ella's breathing is fast, shallow. She needs what every sub needs after a punishment. There's a moment, a moment that's far too short yet suspended in time. And in it, I forget my words. I forget everything except for the way she looks at me.

"Did I do okay?" Her voice quavers, and it's so raw, this thing between us. It's so necessary. And for once I can give a person what they need. For once I'm in the right place at the right time.

I brush her hair behind her back and then run my thumb down the curve of her neck. "You did so well, little bird. That's why I'm going to reward you. Spread your legs wider."

This is for her. But I'd be lying if I said it wasn't also for me.

Her legs are spread over my thighs and I pull her in closer, her forehead resting against the side of my neck. Her body collapses into mine, melting, and I take that moment to skim a hand between her parted thighs and find the heat between her legs.

Ella moans softly and spreads her legs another inch to give me better access. With a rough chuckle, I comment in a low voice full of approval, "Greedy girl."

She's wet. Ready. I don't make her wait long. I push two thick fingers into her without hesitation and she clenches around me. At first she arches her back, and her blunt fingernails dig into my shoulders.

"Steady yourself and fuck my hand." As she does, I make sure I keep my thumb pressed against her clit. I want her to have all the pleasure after getting through her first punishment so well.

Her hips settle into an immediate rhythm, rocking against me, seeking that pleasure. Seeking reward.

"You can have it, little bird. Take it."

"Please," she begs into the crook of my neck, her hips working to fuck my fingers. "Please just let me have you. I want all of you." She stops her movements. "I want you," she emphasizes. She wants my cock inside of her and I'd be damned if I didn't want the same.

I wrap a hand around the back of her neck. "No." It hurts to deny her, but I have to. I'm firm about this. "Take what I'm giving you like a good girl."

I press a thumb to her clit. Three circles. That's all it takes and she's driving her hips forward, fucking my fingers like a wild thing, her face hot on my neck. She comes hard in a series of pulses and flutters around my fingers that I would give anything, anything to feel around my cock.

"Good," I whisper into her ear. "Good girl."

CHAPTER 17

ZANDER

In the event a client requires more specialized care,
alternate methods may be considered.

If I'd had more time, I would feel more prepared to bring her here. Instead, I ask her once again, "What is your signal?"

My sweet submissive, sweet but defiant, lifts three fingers directly over her lips, the tip of her middle finger resting on the tip of her nose. It would be an unnatural response to yawn, given how straight her hand is and exactly perpendicular to her lips. It is our signal. If she gives it, I will immediately interfere and the conversation will halt.

That is the best I can offer her for when the inevitable questions arise.

For her sake, and her beautiful and susceptible heart, I hope it doesn't happen today. Because she's done nothing but smile all morning when "brunch" was mentioned.

Relaxing the tension in my shoulders, I take a moment, praying that she's right about her friends. I can't control what they say or ask or do. So much is out of my control and I don't fucking like it. If it weren't for the fact that this is my job, I would order her not to attend. It's far too soon in our relationship, but this is not my decision and I already knew our arrangement would come with difficulties.

The restaurant her friends chose is upscale and intimate. We climb the rustic paved steps to the upper floor and enter a sunny room bathed in the golden midmorning sun of autumn. From this height, the picture windows are filled with fall colors. The trees on the low mountain rises have leaves in deep red and orange, with flares of yellow. It's a breathtaking view.

The sight reinforces the stark contrast of the worlds we live in. A woman like Ella will have brunch dates and parties to attend, rubbing elbows with the rich and making appearances for charity. She's a high-profile client for a reason. Her wealth is something I'd nearly forgotten until this morning.

This is her reentering her life. The one she left behind. As I follow behind her, only escorting her for support, Damon texts that he's arrived. He's parked outside next to my BMW 760Li. We each have one assigned to us from The Firm.

Black, steel paneled. The security vehicles are unnecessary for Ella, but she did enjoy the leather interior. The car, given to me for the job, is the only piece of luxury I could ever offer her. The thought hits me only now.

"Okay," Ella says and breathes out slowly as she stares at a table in the corner, slipping her periwinkle wool coat down her shoulders. I help her to remove it, but she doesn't let me take it. Instead she holds the folded garment a minute longer, as if it's a shield. Two beautiful women are seated at the farthest end, both smiling and laughing, both oblivious for the moment that Ella's here.

Ella's chest rises and falls with anticipation and I offer her a slight push with my hand on the small of her back. That's the only nudge I give her before her friends notice her and squeal in delight, the chairs pushing back and scraping against the farmhouse wood floors.

With Ella smiling broadly, and quickly joining the women, I text Damon back that we're in location.

Ella described each of her friends to me on the way over. Kelly's the shorter of the two—Asian, with shiny black hair that cascades down to her lower back and the kind of face that belongs in magazines. Her face lights up at the sight of Ella. Trish is tall and blond and wears a playful grin that wouldn't be out of place at a club. From what Ella said, she spends a lot of time partying. Together they all look young, rich and carefree. For the moment.

These are her best friends. Her oldest friends. But I know how it is to go back to the world after you've been away, whether it's mentally or physically. Overwhelming as fuck.

With some friends you can pick up where you left off easily, but even if they're those kinds of friends, where Ella left off is ... well, that's where the problem lies. And why I stay on edge, even if her posture confirms that Ella is full of relief and joy.

"Hi," Kelly says, and she wraps Ella into an instant hug. "We missed you."

"We did. So damn much!" Trish wraps her arms around both of them, and Ella is almost lost in the embraces of her friends. "I'm so glad to see you, El. It's been way too long."

Ella clears her throat. "I know."

Kelly blinks; it's only a half second of a response before Kelly corrects her expression. That's the only reaction to the changed sound of her voice.

"Sit, sit, sit," she ushers Ella, pulling out a chair for her and Trish pipes up with, "I was just telling Kelly all about the new guy." They move on without addressing it at all. The atmosphere is lighthearted, the women all smiling still.

It's immediately obvious that these women might not know the full story, but they're not going to push her beyond what she can handle. "Let's sit," Kelly says, giving Ella a last pat on the back. "Let's eat."

"I'm all for that," Ella says and laughs. As they take their seats, I search for a waiter or waitress to ask if I can plant myself in the corner of the room, remaining in sight, but at a distance.

"This one is for you," Trish calls out to me. Half-seated, she perks right back up. "There are four chairs for a reason."

"Come, come." Kelly gestures with her hand, waving me over. "I promise we won't bite," she adds.

Trish side-eyes her with a devilish smile before turning that grin to Ella and saying loud enough for me to hear, "Shh, don't tell him Kelly's lying."

Ella doesn't miss a beat laughing along with the girls and she turns in her seat, brimming with a happiness I have yet to see her wear back at her home. It's a striking contrast and when she asks politely, "Please, would you sit with us," but with wide pleading eyes, I offer her the professional response.

"This is your brunch—"

"Oh no, we insist," Kelly interjects. Clearing my throat, I give them a tight smile and take the seat next to Ella. Heat races along the back of my shoulders. This is what we would do for any other client, I remind myself. This is professional. That is all this is.

Ella's gaze burns into me and rather than looking, rather than giving our relationship away, I reassure her that all is well by slipping my hand onto her thigh. Balancing the professional image with the very unprofessional touch. With it, though, Ella laughs. "You two practically bullied him," she teases.

As Kelly shamelessly shrugs, Trish leads the conversation.

"So." Trish picks up her water goblet and takes a sip. "Who's this, El?"

For a split second, Ella beams at me. It sets my heart racing. Then her expression settles into something more neutral. Good. "This is Zander, one of the men from the private firm I hired."

This is the story we've settled on for when Ella makes these appearances—that she's hired a new security firm. No one else needs to know the details, and no one ever will. The Firm prides itself on confidentiality. "It's nice to meet you ladies," I say to greet them.

Trish shares a look with Kelly, who raises her eyebrows. It's over in the blink of an eye, and I sit back in my seat and stay quiet. It's not long before the three women are talking around me.

This is exactly what I want.

I'm here to observe Ella for signs that she needs to leave, whether it's with her signal or otherwise, and that is all.

Watching her with her friends is a stark difference from the silent woman in the courtroom almost a month ago. She is different with Kam, more laid back and less high energy than she is now with her friends. She is dynamically beautiful, transparently confident, and yet, when no one is looking ... I know she has her moments. We all do.

The conversation is easy and light, as are the meals the

women eat. The brunch consists of dainty pastries, a variety of fresh fruits and berries, eggs benedict and sides of bacon, sausage and ham.

Although the women are slim, the platters disappear quickly and I half wonder where they put it away. Ella herself doesn't hesitate to take her share and when the women push it on me to eat, I do so for politeness only.

A half an hour passes without the women concerning themselves with me at all.

Kelly tells Ella about a book she read—apparently she likes fantasy, and she likes it steamy—and only once does she cut a glance at me. "Sorry, Zander," she says, and Ella laughs.

I offer a smirk, again telling myself it's to be polite, although I will admit, I'm fond of the way they treat Ella. Trish whispers, "I bet Z would like it," "there's totally sex in it." Kelly laughs as Trish asks Ella, "What do you think?"

"If I had time to read, maybe I could offer an opinion."

"Oh?" Now Trish is looking at me, and I don't mind it, not exactly. I prefer my focus to remain on Ella, though. "Is this one keeping you busy?"

Heat blazes along the back of my neck and my right hand flexes. It's one of the signals, commanding Ella to behave.

I see an echo of that woman from the videos on the porn site. Not the woman on her social platforms who shared her day-in, day-out life with her followers, but the vixen at night. Her kinky, her less sweet, and much more provocative side.

Ella's gaze falls to my hand, and I rest a loose fist on the table.

"I saw the comments, but that's not what this is."

"Oh," Kelly says and pouts, but Trish doesn't seem to accept it, judging by the way her gaze dances between us.

"I am here only to do my job. I'm sorry to disappoint you."

Ella's reaction is tense at first. I imagine she's wondering now whether she's been behaving or not. The slight flush on her beautiful cheeks gives it away. It takes her quite a few minutes to relax her shoulders and settle into the rhythm again as the women order cappuccinos and lattes. It doesn't go unnoticed that they're quick to turn down the mimosas the waiter offers.

Time ticks by even after the dishes are removed. I don't care if we sit here until the restaurant closes, if that's what Ella wants to do.

Kelly has a constant stream of things to talk about, and Trish chimes in, the two of them a perfect team of entertainment and ease. Ella joins in from time to time. Occasionally her fingers tap her throat and she quickly sips her ice water to squelch whatever pain has come. This may be the first time she's spoken for so long and so loudly. She generally keeps her voice low with me, but it's not at all here. She doesn't say as much as her friends, but it still doesn't seem like they're overpowering her. It's like the three of them are a unit. They know when to give and take.

I like that for her. I didn't expect to feel so relieved when her friends turned out to be good people. There's a sense of jealousy there too—that these women know Ella in a way I might never understand. They knew her before and she has yet to share that with me.

I'm watching Ella's face so intently that I miss the change in the conversation.

"—like James used to do."

Her gaze drops down to the tea bag that sits on the edge of a small porcelain saucer, the smile still in place on her face. "Mm-hmm," she answers.

Trish is still speaking, but I lose the rest entirely. It doesn't matter. Ella runs her fingers through the napkin in her lap and raises her head to continue with the conversation.

I abandon all thoughts of anything other than signs of distress, staying relaxed. I'm not going to give her friends any indication there's a problem—especially if there isn't one yet.

At first I think Ella's lifting her hand to touch her throat again, my body tense and waiting still. But then her fingertips hover over her lips.

My reaction is instant. I take out my phone and study the screen. "I need to step outside for a moment." I speak over Kelly, effectively halting the conversation, saying it with a smile, and Trish and Kelly both smile back. "Ella, would you come with me?" I don't dare glance at the other women, although their objections come with a short gasp from one of the two of them. She nods gratefully, not speaking, and I pull out her chair for her to stand. In her silence, I promise the women, "I'll bring her back in a few minutes."

"You'd better," scolds Trish. It's not lost on me that the two don't speak while we leave. Which is certainly an indication that they will the moment we're off.

With a hand on Ella's lower back, I escort her out of the restaurant. Silently we descend the stairs, although her pace is quicker than my own. She turns immediately to the right and heads through a small alley that lets out to a riverwalk. The river in autumn reflects the colors of the trees, and Ella walks without hesitation to the railing and leans against it.

I should take my hand off her back.

I don't.

Ella lifts her head and peeks at me. "I'm not going to jump."

I think she means it as a joke, but I answer the emotion in her eyes instead of the words. "You're thinking about that? Is that where your head has gone?"

She shakes her head. "No. But I was worried yours might be there."

I assure her, "It's not. And you would fail miserably if you attempted to jump while I was here."

She huffs a small laugh with a smile that doesn't reach her eyes as she gazes over the still waters.

"I just needed some fresh air." She touches the front of her chest, and I know. I know that feeling. Someone says a name you're not expecting and you have a small heart attack. Hurts like the muscle itself has been bruised. I know it so well.

I hate this moment. This grief that she's coping with. But to deal with it in such a healthy way, I admire her. "I am proud of you," I tell her and she peers up at me.

"I couldn't even last a brunch, and you're proud."

"How is this not lasting?" I ask her, pushing back.

"Would you hold me, then? I deserve a reward, don't I?" Her pleas are voiced in a teasing manner, her wide eyes still glinting with vulnerability.

My intention is to pull her in for a hug. But as I reach for her, something else takes over. I don't put my hands on her shoulders. I reach for her face, take her chin in my hand, and pull her to me.

And kiss her.

Right there on the riverwalk.

Ella's lips part for me and she makes a little noise into my mouth, a contented sigh. *Fuck*, she tastes good. Sweet and delectable. I run my tongue along the seam of her lips and she lets me in. It's so easy, and so right, like she was made for me. Like my whole life was dragging me here by the hand.

Boundaries be damned.

My little bird presses close to me, her body warm against mine, and I find both hands in her hair, both hands pulling her in. I don't want her far from me. I don't want her anywhere out of my sight. I want this forever.

And if I'm honest, which I haven't been—not with Cade,

not with Damon, not with myself—I want her so badly it hurts. Kissing her shoves the truth out into broad daylight. Punishing her will never be enough. Making her come will never be enough. A quick, hard fuck would do nothing to kill this craving. With her, it wouldn't stop until I'd had my fill. Until I'd tasted each of her boundaries and all her sadness and let her see mine as well. Let her tear them all down.

Ella kisses me back, harder than before, and then she comes up for air. It tastes sweet and crisp, like this autumn breeze. But nothing is as sweet as her arms around my neck. She leans back into my hands, trusting me to hold her up.

"Z," she whispers.

"Little bird."

I untangle her arms from my neck, but it's the last thing I want to do. Reality is setting in. We're out behind the brunch restaurant, where anyone could see. I've lost track of time. I have no idea how long I tasted her. How long I lost myself in her mouth and her touch.

"Are you ready?" I question her. I'll be right there beside her with whatever excuse or escape she needs when we return to that table.

"I want to use the restroom before we go back."

"Go ahead," I tell her. "I'll wait for you by the stairs."

She turns my hand in hers so she can press a kiss to my knuckles. "Are you okay?"

"Are you?"

Her grin lifts up the corners of her mouth, and I can't help myself—I press my thumb to that curve and then run it over her cheekbone. "I'm good," Ella says. "I just had a little moment." With a small shake of her head, a laugh gets away from her. "I'd rather stay out here and kiss you. But my friends will wonder where we went."

"Mmm," is all I can say, and my hum of approval is low and deep. *As would I.*

Ella rises on tiptoe and kisses my cheek, a brief heat against my skin, and then she's gone, moving back through the alley.

I'm about to turn around and let the railing keep me from collapsing when I see him.

Damon.

At the corner of the building, his eyes on Ella as she enters the small restroom beside the alley. My heart pounds. Damon comes to a stop a foot in front of me, and when he looks into my eyes, I know.

He saw.

He saw everything.

Damon slips his hands in his pockets, his jaw working. There are probably a hundred things he'd like to say to me right now, and I tense, waiting for the worst of them. How I've put Ella at risk. How I've been dishonest. How I could truly fuck things up for The Firm, and, by extension, for him. The silence gets painful.

The worst of it is that admitting any of it threatens to take her away from me.

There's no judgment in his words, only disapproval in his expression when he states, "You have to tell your brother."

CHAPTER 18

ELLA

While emotional attachments between clients and members of The Firm are expected, these attachments will be carefully managed so they do not compromise the safety of the client or any member of The Firm.

All I keep thinking about is how well it went. I hadn't realized how much I missed them. I missed going out, I missed laughing, I missed seeing the people I love.

There's still a pounding anxiousness in my chest that won't quit. It's been there since this morning and it hasn't left me for a moment, other than one.

When Zander cupped my chin, when he let me deepen the kiss, when he pulled me in close to him and there wasn't a thing separating us.

It all stopped then, and that anxious feeling in my chest ... it changed. It's still there thrumming away as I wait for him at the bottom of the stairs.

Picking at my nails, I wonder if he feels it too. I can't help but to worry. He's been different, quiet. Or at least I think he has. Maybe it's all in my head.

A huff of nervous laughter leaves me at the thought.

Damon took me home after lunch so it's been hours now since I've seen Zander, but he should be here any moment. I imagine he'll be wearing what he did earlier, but I've changed. There's a chill that slips up the silk fabric of my pale pink robe as I sit here and without anything under it, shivers grace my bare skin.

I remember this part. I remember falling. To be in this moment and know it is surreal. That fluttering of butterflies dives lower as the rumble of my name reaches me. His timbre is low, seductive.

"There you are," he murmurs and I peer up at him, sitting on the bottom step and feeling so small beneath him.

He towers over me and I'm so very aware of how much power I've given him. How much control he has over my emotions, my actions ... my desires.

"And there you are," I offer him in return, attempting to maintain a semblance of confidence that seems blurred in all of this.

"I did good today … didn't I?" I question and if I wasn't his submissive, I'd hate that I'm searching for his approval. If I'm honest, part of me isn't at this moment. Part of me sees a man I'm falling for, and I want him to be proud of me.

"You did exceptionally well."

"I told you you'd like them." Nervous jitters leave me as I reach for the journal. "You'll want to read the part I've bookmarked with the ribbon," I tell him and swallow the knot in my throat. "I did what you asked. I wrote what it was that I thought would please you most."

My heart pounds as Zander takes the journal from me, his fingers slipping against mine as he does and there's an electric knowing that forces me to pull my hand away faster than I'd like.

His stubbled jaw is strong at this angle, his gaze holding something I haven't seen before. *Thump*, *thump*, my heart wars inside of me.

"You wrote what would please me most?" he asks and I nearly spill it all right now as I stare up at him, praying he'll understand. That what I feel for him is what he feels for me and that even my darkest days won't take away from what we have.

Tears prick at the memory, the memories, the anguish, the shame still fresh in my mind. "I did it. And you said … you promised that I could pick what would please me most if I did it," I remind him. The desperation in my voice doesn't go unnoticed by either of us.

Letting the hand holding the notebook fall to his side, Zander asks me, "And what is it that you want most? What would please you most?"

Standing on shaky legs, my fingers fumble with the tie of the robe, but only for a half second before it comes undone. The moment it opens, I shrug it off my shoulders and let the diaphanous fabric fall to the floor, leaving me bared to him.

His gaze drops to my breasts and he utters my name in weakness, "Ella."

"Take me," I plead. "Take me upstairs and make me yours. Please." My fantasy, what I want most ... it's for me to have him, fully and in every way. Not just for tonight, but we can start with this moment.

Staring into his eyes, I pray he can feel how much I need this, especially after today and whatever's changed between us. "I want you," I whisper.

His lips crash against mine and I moan into his mouth. Loving him, needing him. This. All of this. It's everything that I have been missing.

He takes the stairs two at a time. One arm bracing my bare back, his hand gripping my neck to hold me to him, his other arm wrapped around my ass as tightly as my legs are wrapped around his thighs. I'm barely aware of the world around us, it whips by far too quickly.

The second my back hits the door, there's a click of the

knob being twisted and it opens behind me. Ushering an approving groan from Zander.

I'm on the bed at once, letting out a gasp. Zander's quick to undress himself as I push myself back on the bed.

And then there he is, a hunter at the end of my bed. Crawling toward me, naked, and his cock jutting out, hard and thick. The heat from his body is nearly suffocating. He is everything, and nothing else matters as licks his lower lip and takes a languid lick of my pussy. He doesn't hesitate to dip his tongue into my entrance, causing my back to arch. His large hands wrap around my inner thighs, spreading me and holding me there for him as he moves his lips to my clit and sucks.

If I gave a fuck, I'd be ashamed of the mangled whimper that leaves me, but as it is, I don't hide a thing from him. I want him to know what he does to me.

Kissing up my body, he leaves me wanting. His shoulders are foreboding as he cages me under him. The head of his cock teases my lips.

I'm ready to beg him, the words on the tip of my tongue, but they don't make it out. He slams inside of me without any further warning. The sweet pain of being stretched steals my breath. His gaze pins me as much as his body does while my body attempts to accommodate him.

He stays there buried inside of me, ever my ruthless Dominant, while I can barely survive beneath him.

Lowering his lips to mine, he kisses me, sucking in my bottom lip as he pulls out slightly and then pushes himself all the way back in. The movement forces me to hold on to him.

He nips the lobe of my ear and groans, "I knew you'd feel like this ... fucking perfect."

Pulling back, he looks deep in my eyes and tells me, "I wanted to be controlled for you, I wanted to take it slow." My breath is shuddery as he warns me, "But I'm not going to be able to do that this time." Before I can respond, Zander lifts my hips slightly and well and truly fucks me.

I wanted him to take me, and that's exactly what he does.

Pounding into me as if he needs me as much as I need him.

I shatter beneath him. My blunt nails dig into his shoulders and my body tenses around him. With my head thrown back, I'm lost in pleasure. Zander doesn't stop, he rides through my orgasm and every thrust brushes against my clit, heightening the overwhelming bliss.

The sounds of flesh hitting flesh intensify as my arousal spreads between us. It seems to only spur him on, to fuck me hard and faster, to take from me over and over again. I writhe under him as the intensity climbs again, the cliff I'll fall from seemingly higher.

I can barely breathe as the next crashes through me and my neck arches. With the chill of the air hitting my heated face, I scream out his name as my body tenses and every nerve ending blazes. It starts from the pit of my belly and then rages outward.

Zander sucks and nibbles my neck, as I do everything I can to get a grip, to come back down from the highest high. But I can't. His hips piston relentlessly, never giving me a moment to gather purchase. Instead, he kisses me, he fucks me, and his grip keeps me pinned beneath him, leaving me without any mercy at all.

"Zander." His name is a plea on my lips, one he doesn't take. Repositioning my leg higher up, he slams into me, groaning his pleasure into the crook of my neck. I can't help but to cry out my scream of pleasure as he fucks me deeper. Clawing at his back, the mix of pain and pleasure threatens to destroy me. To ruin me.

I try to plead with him, to call out his name. "Z" is barely a whisper as his pace picks up.

Pink. I nearly cry out pink as he thrusts himself inside of me and leaves himself there, his cock pulsing as yet another orgasm paralyzes me.

My heart hammers and my body trembles. It takes me far too long to release, and he's finished with me that time. Leaving my legs shaking. With his forearms braced on either side of my head, he whispers kisses along my jaw and then down my neck, leaving a trail of goosebumps in his wake.

If I could find my voice, I'd tell him he wrecked me. I've had sex plenty throughout my life, although it's been so long now. I've had lovers and one-night stands; I've had a Dom and a husband who loved me and fucked me thoroughly.

This, though, this shattering and feeling bared in a way that's far too vulnerable … This feels like the first time. It feels like Zander's taken something from me I didn't realize I had to give.

He commands me to spread my legs for him, and I do, although they still tremble. He cleans me and I can barely hear him, his shadow moving across the room and then to the bathroom. Turning to my side, I curl up and still, I can't steady myself.

It feels as if everything has changed. It was so slow this morning, so slow for weeks, and then it happened. In a single moment. He took me there and I know there's no going back.

He climbs back into bed, the frame groaning from his weight. The covers rustle as he lays behind me and then pulls me in close to him. The tip of his nose runs along the curve of my neck, his hand gripping my hip. He leaves a chaste kiss just under the shell of my ear and with the shiver of desire running down my body, I'm reminded of how sore he's left me.

"Zander," I whisper his name, still breathless, still unable to move just yet. His lips are pressed against my hair and he kisses me there before that deep, rough hum rumbles up his chest.

Without turning to face him, without having that much courage I tell him, "I think I want more than to just be your client …" My cadence is shaky when I add, not daring to close my eyes, "I want more than to just be your submissive."

There's a beat and then another beat of silence. And then another. Too much time passes with him still behind me, not moving, not saying a word. Betrayal grips my heart and fears run rampant in the back of my mind.

"We have what we have right now, Ella."

He says Ella, not "little bird."

I only nod, my cheek still firm against the pillow. It takes great effort not to let on how much it hurts. How much pain sits against my chest.

We have what we have. Those are not the words of a man who feels the same as what I feel. I remember falling … and I remember heartbreak just as well.

CHAPTER 19

ZANDER

Any misconduct by a member of The Firm will be investigated immediately.

Sleeping with Ella breaks down a wall inside me.

It's all I can think about. And on this drive back to the motel, it's killing me.

I slept with her. I didn't tell my brother. At this point, I don't know that I will. Damon wouldn't betray me. I'd be a shitty person to put him in that position, but if it's for Ella, I'll draw that line.

Everything is so fucked. And my little bird has no idea.

Selfishly I know I've failed her, but I wouldn't change

it. I want to hold on just a while longer, feeling those walls break down.

It's been crumbling for a while now. Probably since the day I saw her standing at the front of that courtroom. Probably since the first time her eyes met mine. On some level, far below conscious thought, I knew I wanted her. All of her.

And I knew it would be different.

It is different.

It has to be different.

My mind can't settle. It's been a runaway mess since I got up from Ella's bed this morning. There was so much rightness in laying her down in her bed, in fucking her like both of us wanted for so long. Peace, like I haven't felt at any point in my life. And then the heartbroken expression on her face. The tears gathering in her eyes.

And the things she said—

They remind me of Quincy.

That combined with Damon texting me, reminding me that I need to be careful. He says he's worried for me.

It's too much like Quincy, man.

The hearing's coming up. I'm worried for you.

You sure this is for the right reasons?

She could get hurt, and you might not see it coming.

It fucking guts me, to second-guess what I feel for her and what I know she feels for me.

Memories from the past keep sneaking up on me.

Quincy's face across the table from me at a wine bar in the city, her blue eyes bright with flirtation and confidence. The disappointment that stared back at me on a street corner, her hand on my chest, those same blue eyes filled with crushing disappointment.

Even now I feel the push as she shoved me away.

Quincy saying, "No. I'm going for a walk. Don't follow me."

I should have followed, but her final statement kept me from trailing after her: "If you don't want all of me, then I don't want any of you."

She was my submissive, but she wanted more. She wanted a "real" relationship.

I hadn't followed her, because she wanted space—and because she wanted something from me that I couldn't give her. What was the point of following, when there was no agreeing to disagree? I didn't want to marry her. I loved her in a way that wasn't that. I broke her heart that night, but it was the truth. She knew when we started that I wasn't looking for more. She said she wasn't either.

She wanted things to progress past sharing an apartment that I barely slept in. Quincy wanted more commitment than a one-year lease. She wanted a ring on her finger, and I couldn't do it.

Not because I didn't love her. I did, in a way. But not in the way I feel about Ella. It was the way you care about a person when you're trying to give them what you want, at the expense of giving up what you need.

Quincy wanted me to be different for her.

Ella just wants me to be hers.

Fuck, it hurts.   The worst part of it all is that I am questioning everything.   Does Ella truly want to be with me? Or did I take advantage of a young woman who would have clung to whoever had been there for her first?

The migraine combined with the sleepless night is too much as I turn onto the drive.

If she has the same feelings for me as I do for her, then I have to fix this.

It's like a lightning strike, and I'm turning the wheel before I can think about it.   Braking.   Throwing it into reverse.   I'm going back.

If Ella feels that way about me, then I have to make it right, and I have to do it now.   I have to hold on to her the way she deserves.

I'm not far away.   It won't be long until I can fix this.

Ella's house appears on the side of the road out of nowhere.   I'm not aware of the route I took, or anything else. I'm only aware of a fierce pounding in my heart and a twist in my gut.

Again I question myself.

Did I take advantage of her last night?

Did I take advantage of her pain and her desires?   Or is all of this meant to be and it's just a fucked-up situation that brought us together?

I only wish I could pause. To take in every detail. To make sure she's all right. To ensure that whatever I do next, is best for her.

Quincy left me that night, and I let her. I let her walk away. What happened next was a tragedy and I've never regretted anything more. If I could go back, I would change it all.

I let her walk home alone while I went the other way. I knew it wasn't safe. Nearly midnight on the city streets. I knew I should have followed her.

But then again, I knew I should have ended it with her weeks before.

I will never forgive myself if Ella doesn't make it out of this well and whole.

I can't be wrong again. I pull into my spot behind the house. One, two, three, four. Again I repeat the breaths. Again. Until I'm calm enough to focus. Until I'm calm enough to walk inside and make this right.

The answers aren't hiding behind my steering wheel. The answers can only be found by seeing this through.

Then Damon comes out the back door with his coat on. Alone.

He sees me, and the corners of his mouth turn down.

And then I'm out of the car, heading for him.

His jaw is hard, the clean cut of his button-down combined with how his shoulders straighten and he stares me down as I approach. Like we're squaring up for a fight. "You didn't tell him," Damon speaks low and deliberately. "You're my friend, but I can't let you do this."

"No, I didn't tell him. I'm coming here to talk to you."

"It's too late."

Betrayal feels like a hot knife in my gut. "You didn't," I grit out from between clenched teeth. "You didn't fucking tell him, Damon. You didn't."

He only stares back at me.

"Why are you out here?" It's too much to come clean to him now, with this storm in my chest. "Is somebody else in there with her?"

Damon shakes his head. "There's nobody inside."

"What the fuck? You know we can't—"

"There's *nobody* inside."

It sinks in then, what he means. I grab for the front of his jacket on instinct but Damon's as strong as I am, and he gets me around the wrist. "You did this."

"I didn't tell him shit. It wasn't me." I let him go and run for the kitchen door. Throw it open. Go inside.

"Ella," I call out.

The house is empty.

I know it, because I can sense it, because it's my job to know. I know this stillness.

I look anyway.

The sitting room is both dark and quiet, without the lit

fire, without her waiting there with her gorgeous dark gaze giving me a longing that echoes within myself.

Anger and regret are a bitter thing to swallow. I take the stairs two at a time, checking her bedroom, the guest room, everywhere. It still smells like her up here. I was only gone for twenty minutes. I run back down and grip the doorframe at the sitting room. She's not here. It's empty.

She's not here.

Damon's footsteps stop close by.

"Kamden had suspicions," he says from behind me, an edge in his voice so hard I don't dare look at him. I can't. "He put cameras in the house, Zander. They know."

Dread washes over me. But Damon doesn't stop talking.

"Caleb and Ella are with him now. There may be an emergency hearing." He's pissed. At me.

"Cameras—more than the ones we installed?"

"Yes."

I finally face him. Anger and desolation stare back at me. "Everybody knows what happened." A deep breath. "You're being removed. You aren't allowed to see her again."

My own rage boils over. "You're not going to keep me from her. Whatever you said, whatever you did, you fucked this up—"

Damon stabs a finger into my chest. "*You* fucked this up, Z. You crossed a line. You hid it from everybody. You could have hurt her. You could be taking us all down, so don't try to blame me for your own stupid mistakes."

"You can't do this." I don't know if I'm talking to him or myself. "You can't take her from me."

My oldest friend huffs out a breath and straightens his jacket, disappointment rolling off him in waves. "I didn't do this. You did. Look me in the eye right now." I do it, and he returns my gaze, furious and hurt. When he speaks, it's with an icy clarity. "It's over. For good."

The National Suicide Prevention Lifeline is a United States-based suicide prevention network of over 160 crisis centers that provides 24/7 service via a toll-free hotline at the number 1-800-273-8255. It is available to anyone in suicidal crisis or emotional distress.

About the Authors

Willow Winters

Thank you so much for reading my romances. I'm just a stay at home Mom and an avid reader turned Author and I couldn't be happier.

I hope you love my books as much as I do!

More by Willow Winters
www.willowwinterswrites.com/books

Amelia Wilde

USA today bestselling author of dangerous contemporary romance and loves it a little too much. She lives in Michigan with her husband and daughters. She spends most of her time typing furiously on an iPad and appreciating the natural splendor of her home state from where she likes it best: inside.

More by Amelia Wilde
www.awilderomance.com/

Made in United States
Troutdale, OR
09/01/2024